J. E. G.

Songs and Etchings in Shade and Sunshine

J. E. G.

Songs and Etchings in Shade and Sunshine

ISBN/EAN: 9783744746809

Printed in Europe, USA, Canada, Australia, Japan

Cover: Foto ©Andreas Hilbeck / pixelio.de

More available books at **www.hansebooks.com**

Etchings
by
J.E.G.

SONGS AND ETCHINGS

IN

SHADE AND SUNSHINE

By J. E. G.

LONDON:
SAMPSON LOW, MARSTON, SEARLE, & RIVINGTON.
1880.

TO THE CHILDREN OF SONG.

" O Muse, alto 'ngegno hor m' aiutate."
                                        DANTE.

" Es vano á la puerta llama
Quien no llama al corazon."
                            JOSÉ DE IGLESIAS.

A STRANGER tarries at your Golden Gate—
  No mendicant, nor yet with pride elate.
Unknown as yet to your harmonious guild—
Sweet hope of entrance now my soul hath fill'd.
This satchel bears some fragments quaint of rhyme—
The silent language of a lonely time
When, winding through a thorny path, with feet
Oft wounded there, I heard wild carols sweet
Of birds—low fluttering in ambrosial air,
Who straightway bid me to their haunts repair,
Where downy, flow'ry beds invited rest
With lullaby to calm a mind opprest.
The fancy took, forthwith to them I went—
The lone intruder on their merriment.

But who would sleep when nightingales awake?
Nor vigil keep for their rare music's sake?—
So, by the roses on their fragrant bank
I lay and listen'd, then in dreams half sank!
Too soon it ceased; for when the sunbeams rose
Myriads of wings their busy errands chose:
In embassies some flew to honey'd cell,
And hummings faint and chirpings loud would tell
Of life astir—on hill, in dale, by rill,
And me they mock'd that I was silent still.
My thoughts, they seem'd most like to fallen leaves
The frolic wind at random nimbly thieves:
One moment trooping o'er the forest sward,
The next, light, wheeling backward, hitherward,
Then—led away by some elected chief—
All hurrying off in dances strange and brief,
Till, circling some huge trunk that bars the way,
They cling together, and stand there at bay.

Anon, I sought to gather up in verse
My vagrant thoughts, as pastime to rehearse
Journeying on.   Now, to your threshold near,
Can song so poor yet win for me your ear?

L'Espérance me soutient.

CONTENTS.

CONTENTS.

CONTENTS.

THE CARILLON AT CALAIS.

HIGH-CRADLED in the ancient tower
   That looks o'er land and sea,
Through many a year has lurk'd a power
   Weaving a spell o'er me.

Far have I come once more to hear
   Time's herald from aloft
Tell the same tale in chimes so clear,
   And music sad and soft.

I loved that air—I love it yet
   Above all other lays.
Who sang that song—can I forget?
   Or all youth's golden days!

THE CARILLON AT CALAIS.

Although an alien on this shore,
   What matters it to me?
My thoughts to yonder heaven soar—
   My spirit still is free.

To me there's not a spot on earth
   Less friendless than the rest,
For I can clasp amid the dearth
   Bright phantoms to my breast.

Yet it is strange to be alone,
   Last of a loving band
That from Life's portal erst has gone
   So gaily hand in hand!

Oh, Mem'ry! with thy cypress wreath,
   Relentless, firm, and true,
Give back but once the living breath,
   The charm of old renew!

Let me but hear each word again,
   As in fond thought it dwells,
Not greet alone the barren strain
   Of cold and lifeless bells!

There is a pause—but mark the sound
   That follows slowly there:
How Time keeps on his solemn round,
   Nor heeds the things that were!

As evening fades, the shipman's light
   Above the city gleams—
To me there is but cheerless night
   Without the ray of dreams!

The sentinel beside the gate,
    Where deep the shadow falls,
Cannot for morn more eager wait
    Than I within these walls.

My hostelry is strange and drear:
    I fling the casement wide,
And see the masts of vessels near
    That rock upon the tide.

A brief space more, and o'er the deep
    Away I must be sped,
The echo of those chimes to keep
    That link me with the dead !

My native land, my home, are names
    That cling around the past ;
As in the waste some ruin claims
    Remembrance to the last.

There's none to kindle more the spark
    Of welcome to that home,
The ashes on my hearth are dark—
    What marvel if I roam?

MAJORA DE CLAVDE MONET.[1]

[1] Inscription on the dial-plate of the Carillon Clock at Calais.

THE FARANDOLE.

THEY come! they come! they fleetly come,
  So merry and so frolicksome!
O'er the sun-lit path advancing,
As 'twere circling sunbeams dancing,
Hand in hand with song and laughter—
Care will come too soon hereafter—
Vigorous limbs, and shapes whose grace
Proclaims descent from classic race;
Tawny youth and dark-hair'd maid,
Whose eyes light up the soft lid's shade;—
A group that Phidias might have wrought
To life by fire Prometheus brought.

The olive-grove they leave behind
And float their tresses on the wind,
Sweeping onward to the mountain,
Past the pine-trees to the fountain—
Trysting-place of all the Muses—
Where kind Hippocrene diffuses
Inspiring draughts that tempt the lip,
They bend a moment there to sip,
Then onward, onward, still they rush
The dew from off the heath to brush,
And mount unto Apollo's throne,
There homage to the Day is done.

THE FARANDOLE.

And thus they dance the Farandole,
For Mirth deals out no stinted dole,
And Poetry seems all abroad
Scattering from her ample hoard
Every charm to nature known—
A paradise awhile our own !
Ah ! land of beauty, love, and all
That most the senses may enthral,
To think of thee brings back the time
So matchless in thy own bright clime—
When mountain, sea, ere yet 'tis night,
Are flooded o'er with rosy light ;
How stern soe'er our thoughts may be
We turn with smiles to welcome thee !

THE MISER.

THE shadow leaves the dial-stone
Above where sits the miser lone.
His hoards are Memory's fondest gifts,
And from the dust of Time he sifts
Each treasured coin so pure and bright,
And handles it with strange delight
  The gold thus true to find.

Distinct each legend circling round
That long his heart had held spell-bound,
And clearer still, and more prized yet
The features where Love's seal is set—
The effigies of those whose sway
Shall never—cannot pass away—
  The rulers of the mind !

Arouse him not !—You speak in vain—
For him what newer wealth were gain ?
Though others deem it out of date,
To *him* no years its worth abate :
The casket's key by Sorrow given,
Its chain whose links no force hath riven,
  Are with his life entwined.

EROS.

NE morn before a mirror stood
   Eros in full array ;
For once he there in pensive
    mood
   Ceased to disport and play.

He spread his wings, and smiled
   to find
   Some feathers missing were,
And saw how little dim or
    blind
   His bright eyes sparkled there.

His quiver's every golden shaft
   He, laughing, left untried,
With tendrils soft and Flora's craft
   A true-love knot he tied.

"Oh, folly !" the young god exclaim'd,
   "To say Love's swift of wing !
See how his flight his mistress tamed,
   Drawn by her silken string !

EROS.

" They call him blind who sees tenfold
   More fair each charm adored—
Finds beauty when those faults unfold
   That others have deplored."

But Love must be beloved again,
   Not trifled with nor teazed,
And softly bound—unfelt the chain—
   Nor rudely lured and seized:

Then Love will "give the world the lie"—
   'Twas noble Raleigh's strain—
And never more attempt to fly,
   But ever true remain.

ON A PICTURE.

REMEMBER'D scene! thy early charm returns
   With keener power, since now the sad heart mourns
More than Time's wonted change in earthly things,
While to thee changeless that heart fondly clings.
Yes! on thine own enchanting paths I trace
My being's prime, in steps no years efface:
The deep affection nurtured in thy bowers—
Thy sparkling rivulets, thy banks, thy flowers!
I would some star enshrined a rest like thine—
It were still earthly, yet to me divine!

I hear in fancy down thy pictured shore
The warning waves that sigh "No more! no more!"
That shore—it was a region of delight,
Whate'er its aspect—or by day, or night!

And Thought portrays a long-departed pair
Whose haunt it was in stormy days or fair.
Turn where they would enchantment there was found :
They watch'd the white sail of the outward-bound,
Loved the wild sea-bird for its freedom's sake,
And wish'd 'twas theirs to follow in its wake !
A symbol sweet in every trifle sought,
When to their feet the tide its offerings brought.

Wild melodies they sang—by Sirens borne
Down to their caves beyond the waves' rude scorn—
Until the nightingale, within her dell,
Took up the lay and bade the day farewell !
Then came the glory of the sun's last hour,
With all its beauty but its saddening power !

As at kings' feasts, when regal pomp retires,
And myriad lamps put out their colour'd fires,
The guests pass forth into the chilly night,
And all is dark that shone so gay and bright.—
So slowly leaves—when once the signal's given—
The bright array that fill'd the dome of heaven :
Thus ends the monarch's festival on high—
Ah ! who can paint it ere 'tis all gone by ?

THE TROOPER'S WAR-SONG.

THE bugle notes sound,
   On horseback we bound,
Each steed his rider hath found.
                        Hurrah !

Our swords flash like flame
   From scabbards that came,
Onward to lead us to fame.
                        Hurrah !

The battle is nigh,
   We win or we die
To vict'ry's glorious cry.
                        Hurrah !

No cowards are here,
   Nor spirit of fear.
The hour of danger we cheer.
                        Hurrah !

The cannon's fierce roar
Not once shall give o'er
Till foemen rise up no more.

Hurrah !

Our horses are fleet,
The sound of their feet
Is never heard in retreat.

Hurrah !

Then, if we must die,
In honour we'll lie,
With valour none can deny.

Hurrah !

Our souls will belong
To that mighty throng
Which lives in our country's song.

Hurrah !

PÈRE LA CHAISE.

AROUND this hill, above yon plain
    Two rival cities rise,
Distraught by kings who strive to gain
  The mastery they prize.

In silence and by stealth one arms
    Pale as the noon-day moon—
His touch alone, when felt, alarms,
    For darkness follows soon.

Around the other's throne appears
    An ever-moving throng ;
And some with laughter, some in tears,
    Urge Time's swift hours along :

Or, giddy with the nectar draught
    Of beauty, talent, wit,
Fall where the silent sovereign's craft
    Bids flowers veil the pit.

Thus Death, thus Life—each mighty king—
    Fights for a trembling world ;
And through the air their war-cries ring,
    With weapons wildly hurl'd.

How calmly they whose years are o'er
    Sleep 'neath the cypress gloom !
The siren-city sings no more
    To those within the tomb.

THE LAST HOURS OF NIGHT.

I T still is night on earth's and heaven's brow,
   Softly away the hours are stealing now ;
The fallen leaves of autumn's strife have rest,
The gale is not yet roused, and on their breast
The gather'd dew-drops weep o'er their decay,
E'en as we mourn o'er fair things past away !
And in their tears, as oft in ours, there's light,
Celestial light, trembling, yet pure and bright :
A silent message from the stars that's sent
To raise our thoughts too long on sorrow bent,
And kindle Hope's exhausted flame anew,
Dispelling clouds that round it coldly grew.

The moon is darken'd with the shade this world
Casts upon all ! Joy—from her high throne hurl'd
Long ages since—hath found no rest, but flies
Onward and upward, beck'ning to the skies.
All, all is hush'd ; yet when yon waning moon
Shall set, and stars be gone, ah, then, too soon
The slumb'ring human host will stir and arm
For holy warfare, or for cruel harm ;

And some will wake—with thoughts unhallow'd wake—
Deface the beauteous, senseless clamour make,
Let passions loose, and revel in their sway,
Defy their God, and rush their headlong way.
Oh! not for these the truce like this, serene:
Conscience might rise—a spectre on the scene.

It still is night, and Heaven to Earth seems nigh!
No sound, but 'midst the trees the south winds sigh;
Nor bell, nor chime, nor faithful watch-dog's bark
Comes from that city shrouded in the dark;
Not yet the poison'd mist pollutes the air—
Satan's foul incense to his fouler prayer—
His venom'd trail the partial shadow hides,
Baneful and deadly, where he darkly glides.

How beautiful the time!   But for Grief's sting,
In such we'd deem the sons of God did sing
Their blissful song around that glorious shrine
Whence came the Voice that bade those spheres to shine!
Calm hour of peace, if not of sleep's repose,
When Heaven is near, Earth's scenes appear to close.
The soul—its painful search less fetter'd then—
Sighs for release, and dares to whisper " When? "

Yet as I watch, this vision too must fade,
Returning oft, but ever fleeting made.
Ye mimic stars! thou moon! ye mystic orbs!
Your reign well-nigh is o'er!   The sun absorbs,
With slow but conquering march, your tender beams;
Far in the east the coming pageant gleams;

Triumphant flash'd on high his fiery spear,
Behold the Sovereign of the day draws near !
With lingering love the Morning-star still glows :
Now pallid, wan, like passion slighted shows—
Then to her sister-planets tells her tale,
And blooms once more in Night's far-distant vale !

LAMENT TO MY FALCON.

M Y noble bird! now cherish'd long
   With thoughts that to past years belong—
Whence cam'st thou here? and whither fled?
I cannot count thy spirit dead.

Thou wert too beautiful in life
For Death to conquer thee in strife!
Symbol of a bygone time!
When chivalry was in its prime,

And to the wrist of high-born dame
The docile falcon went and came,
And queens and kings on mettled steeds
Rode ambling through Old England's meads,
While tassel-gentil's jingling bells
Resounded down the mossy dells.

Thy presence was of regal state
With meanest things that scorn'd to mate ;
Thy glance could pierce a deeper sky
Than e'er thy lord's far duller eye,
And on the burning disc could look,
And scathless all its radiance brook.
Thou might'st, with flight so swift and bold,
The secrets of the clouds have told :
A wider prison than is mine
Did Nature give to thee and thine.
And yet, brave bird ! with me thou dwelt—
It seem'd captivity unfelt—
And now, imprison'd and alone,
I would with thine *my* life had flown !

Still may I see thee, *Gentil-Bird !*
Where Freedom's deathless voice is heard ;
Thy sojourn with me not forgot,
Though thou hast found a happier lot.
Whate'er thy form, thy soul I'll trace—
Thy trusting and submissive grace—
For thou, my bird, didst love the wild,

Although to serfdom reconciled,
Nor could'st thou that sweet life forget.
Ah ! thou and I—we'll breathe it yet !
And fly together—fly with speed
To *one* who found thee in thy need,
And saved thy life before too late,
Or others left thee to thy fate !
What welcome waits, thou knowest well—
My Falcon !—can I say farewell ?

COLOGNE.

TO Cologne's fanè, so grey and old,
   Revered by Eastern kings,
The jewell'd sceptre, crown of gold,
   No more its pilgrim brings;

The halo superstition set
   Around those antique walls—
Of half its glory though bereft,
   The verger's care recalls:—

And relics which their thousands heal'd—
   Kept under lock and key—
The Magi's gifts—are all reveal'd,
   To sceptics, it may be !

Fair Ursula now breathes again
    From forth the canvas quaint—
Her thousand virgins strive to gain
    A place around their saint.

Van Eyck his talent there displays
    (The first to limn in oil)—
His devotee all stiffly prays
    By his creative toil.

Yet linger not in further search—
    The Dom's rich treasures seen—
Go rather to Saint Peter's church,
    If yet you have not been:

Within that church is found the font
    Where Rubens was baptized,
And o'er the altar's sculptured front
    A masterpiece most prized.

The brightest ray that gilds the fame
    Of this old Rhenish town
Descends from his illustrious name—
    That noble of renown!

The mansion as his birthplace kept,
    A twofold legend bears—
For here a royal exile wept,
    Here closed her hapless years.

THE PRIEST AND THE PENITENT.

A MAN of God is on his way—
He heeds such summons night and day—
To shrive a poor departing ghost
In presence of the Sacred Host.

The penitent, will he declare
Each sin, nor shrink the task to dare?
Oh, tell me, Priest, if that you can,
How each misdeed of life you scan?

Methinks 'tis not for thee the task—
My boldness pardon thus to ask!—
What Priest with mimic crown of thorns
And garb, that cloth of gold adorns—

What Cardinal in scarlet robe
  Can hope the heart's recess to probe?—
What thrice-crown'd Pope hath eye or ear
  Man's depth of crime to see or hear?

Oh! He alone whose Spirit sent
  Its breath to this frail tenement—
He knows alone a mortal's power,
  And kens man's worth in trial's hour.

IN THE CHURCHYARD OF STRATFORD-ON-AVON.

WITH saunt'ring steps and thoughts that range
   Through charms of verse that never change,
I enter precincts holy made
   By their sweet singer's haunting shade.

Enchantment round me newly breathes,
   And coronals the memory wreathes
Wherever faintest trace can say,
   " Thus did it look in Shakespeare's day !"

Heaven gave to him celestial fire—
   Prometheus' theft that roused Jove's ire—
Yet, throned with stars, he loved not less
   Earth's meekest flower's loveliness.

Across the mead come notes astray
   That Philomel's soft plaint betray—
Tuneful ever, and ever sad,
   As though she fain could not be glad.

E

It seems to tell the tearful tale
   Of something missing in the dale—
All vaguely heard—yet strangely clear
   To hearkening sympathetic ear.

And as I muse, with vanish'd smile,
   An anthem peals from forth yon aisle,
'Midst the tombstones slowly dying,
   To my soul 'tis thus replying:

" Our brother came to trouble born—
   Life's shadows creep beneath its morn:
Who to prolong the light may claim,
   And fan the fainting, sinking flame?"

That chant hath ceased—from whence it rose
   There comes no guidance to disclose:
Yon sacred fane in solemn state
   Untenanted, and fast each gate.

Night's herald through the zenith past,
   As sounds of day retreat at last ;
All things prepare for welcome rest,
   In pallid Twilight's raiment drest.

The choughs no longer wheel around
   Their avenue ; and on the ground
Long shadows warn that coming eve
   The witching spot doth bid me leave !

Resign'd to him was Nature's key
   Of her exhaustless treasury:
What truths or fancies forth he brings
   From unknown depths of secret springs!

His sadder mood for me hath sway—
   Mirth's laughter sooner dies away—
And soothing is this walk beside
   The well-known river's silent tide,—

As gliding on it leaves no trace
   Of time, that runs a rival race—
A glass whose surface marks no change,
   Whate'er the forms that o'er it range.

The martlet's wing is doubled there
   As sky and flood united were,
While blossoms on its sedgy banks
   Find mates beneath in trembling ranks.

A FRAGMENT.

THE revels pass'd—and o'er Parnassus lay
   Such calm as follows passion wept away.
Where ruled the feast, of late so madly wild,
Almost to sadness seem'd the scene beguiled.

Hyperion fled, and Luna's vanish'd beam
Embraced no more by Naiad's sleepless stream,
One only star on Orient's favour'd brow
Shed all the radiance that enchanted now !

Urania's startled vision fail'd to own
That star in spheres where every orb was known.
No meteor's blaze was this, by vapours lit,
In falling splendour through the air to flit !

There came a sense of passing forms above—
Unseen procession of adoring love :
It quivering swept the sad Ægean deep,
Till length'ning space refused those strains to keep.

Faint waned the hymn on Græcia's list'ning shore ;
Then, Echo fail'd to give one cadence more :
Yet each Muse linger'd, and each Grace, still near—
The rapture theirs that blends with joy its tear.

The cycles fade—with Time's unheeded ghosts
That once with glory led their mighty hosts—
The sacred fire—the watchful vestal's flame—
Have perish'd all—remember'd but in name.

Not so that Light the Eastern Sages hail'd—
The Beacon burns—though darkness hath assail'd—
Guiding through elements of bitter strife
To bliss immortal and to deathless life.

Oblivion's icy shroud, that folds around
Those myriad memories to Lethe bound,
Falls here like glacier from the Alpine height,
When cloudless rays pour forth resistless might.

If silent Earth no greeting carol sing,
Swift touch of seraph's wing would music bring—
Then, songs, like wreaths of incense, fill the air,
And heaven-ward float, like softly whisper'd prayer.

Through streaks of dawn—as from Æolian lyres—
There breathes sweet harmony while Night expires ;
And now, with thee, pale Night ! farewell my lay,
Already his—the Harbinger of Day !

TO ———.

ONCE again we have met, far away from that scene
    In childhood and youth so surpassingly fair—
When existence for us wore that aspect serene—
    The mask that adorns ere it changeth to care!

The song of Hispania, or troubadour's sonnet—
    The lays of the Cid, or of Bayard the brave—
How oft would their echoes, when the daylight had set,
    Unite with the sound of the far-rolling wave!

Never more in that home will be heard the guitar
    That blent with a voice in its early fresh power;
There is no serenade to hail Eve's fairest star,
    The night-dews are weeping within the lone bower.

O'er our thoughts, for a moment, the past came again,
    A tear to the smile of our welcome drew near:
When we parted, I joy'd that with you would remain
    The smile left alone—while I shelter'd the tear.

THE OLD FARMER'S TALE.

THAT moss-grown house beside the mill,
  Those acres that my ploughshares till,
Were held, or ere they mine became,
By yeomen of an honour'd name,
      A long time ago!

Now threescore years and ten are mine,
And, like the day, I slow decline,
While thinking on the times gone by—
The busy days that seem'd to fly,
      A long time ago!

When thrifty wives and lasses neat
Spared neither hands nor tripping feet,
And rustic ditties they could sing
Around the hearth at evening,
      A long time ago!

Our autumn feast, how gay it went!
A merry laugh of heart's content
The young, the old, they gave to me—
I then was paramount, you see,
      A long time ago!

Ah ! know you, sir ?—and you may smile—
Remember, I am *old* the while—
The ruddy harvest-moon did seem
For me to wear a brighter gleam,
          A long time ago !

I saw its light in Mary's eyes
What time she talk'd about the skies—
That sweet eve we sat together,
Ere the clouds began to gather,
          A long time ago !

Belike, sir, you yourself have known
A sweet bird from the dovecot flown,
And of the rest ta'en little count,
When far away you saw her mount—
          A long time ago !

Aweary now, my steps are weak,
Yet through yon lytch-gate oft they seek,
'Neath shadow of the drooping yew,
A letter'd stone—that tomb was new
          A long time ago !

My mother sleeps beside the thorn—
But *one* who died in life's pure morn
Awaits me where my heirs shall say,
" Her lover true join'd her one day—
          A long time ago ! "

THE DUEL.

THE gauntlet was thrown, and two warriors stood
    In the glare of defiant hate :
They ceased o'er their wrongs in silence to brood—
    They fought at the mercy of Fate.

The flash of their swords, like flames of the storm,
    Clave the air, on destruction sent ;
Dark rose 'gainst the sky each towering form,
    For wan were the gleams the moon lent.

    *   *   *   *

    *   *   *   *

The dayspring appears on the silent moor,
    A stain on the bracken is seen;
Aloft in the mist the proud eagles soar,
    Above where the combat hath been.

F

Ah! who hither comes to adorn that heap
    Of armour all riven and red ?—
Like some rose laid adown, by them who weep,
    On the bier of the loved and the dead !

No crimson hath streak'd the fair youthful hue,
    Unblanch'd are those dark waves of hair ;
Too swiftly came Death, and his javelin threw,
    Ere reach'd them the touch of despair.

White is the robe that softly enfolds her—
    Once woven to deck a young bride,
It now is her shroud in that sepulchre
    Where sleeps all her joy—and her pride.

LINES ON A HAND FOUND IN WRAITH'S BAY.

DARK flows the tide along the Spirit's Bay,
 And still the storm lives through the murky day,
The night of clamour and the lurid morn
Foretold ill news, by truth or rumour borne.
Red broke the dawn where must'ring clouds, heap'd high
In heavy masses, gather'd slowly nigh ;
Then, lightning's flash announced their march begun—
They speed like warriors who to battle run.
Loud peals the thunder !—proudly marshall'd on,
They fill the sky ; and now the sun is gone.

Fierce on the Isle's inhospitable shore
Th' Atlantic spends its rage in sullen roar ;
And rugged cliffs, where Echo holds her reign,
Send back the challenge to the angry main ;
Ill-omen'd birds, affrighted, fleeing past,
Stretch their black plumes before the howling blast.

Hark ! a cry pierced the tempest-laden air !
Whence comes that cry ?—from horror or despair ?
Rides Death abroad to wake the sleeping world,
His crimson banner on the gale unfurl'd ?—
No vessels in the wide expanse appear
Whence danger's signal could have reach'd the ear.
Whate'er its mission, now that sound is still,
The gale still onward rushes fierce and shrill.

What throws the turbid surf upon the strand ?
A relic strange !—Behold a human hand !
Why hither flung, denies the froward deep
This poor memorial of her dead to keep ?
In shame or pity unto earth restored
From forth the booty which its waters hoard ?
Did murder stain it with the purple dye
In secret shed, but not unknown to lie ?
Dragg'd by avenging wrath to light again,
Bears it a part in God's dread curse to Cain ?
Was that alarm—which hither came and went,
Ere to the beach the sever'd limb was sent—
The spirit's shriek, whom conscience smote unseen,
Aroused to terror by th' unlook'd-for scene,
Condemn'd to haunt that bay, and vainly groan
O'er deeds unhallow'd, useless to bemoan ?

Yet Charity hath nobler thoughts than this,
Forbears to judge if man hath done amiss,
Still less condemn his actions when unknown ;
But round them sheds a radiance of her own.

We'll think that hand could welcome warmly give,
And feel the answer that bid Hope to live,
When, clasp'd in hers whose early love he sought,
His faith and truth to her as offerings brought,
For her awoke the chords, whose notes so well
Might seem to sound its own prophetic knell;
As o'er the minstrel there might then have past
A nameless shadow that near Death forecast.

Oft on his breast, may-be, 'twas cross'd in prayer,
For blessings still his soul to ask might dare,
While gush'd beneath, his life's impetuous stream
Impell'd to joy in some too dazzling dream!
That limb, perchance, in youth's strong day did wield
The trusty blade, nor to a foeman yield;
With steady grasp and proud, upheld on high
His country's standard waving in the sky;
On tented field, and in the combat's front
The first and foremost to deal death was wont;—
How hath it pass'd to meanest state away—
The Ocean's puppet in its savage play!

Whate'er thy tale, poor hand! on yon lone beach
Thy crumbling bones must soon be left to bleach;
And o'er them there some wanderer may tread,
Nor heed these fragments of the unknown dead.
The form that now betrays thee will not last,
Thy tale already to oblivion past!
Heap'd with the refuse of a fickle sea,
'Midst rotting weed thy lot awhile may be.

Thou art rejected by thy parent Earth,
Albeit to thee she gave ill-fated birth ;
Thy dust, forbade to mingle with her clay,
By wandering breezes shall be snatch'd away,
And, to the ceaseless whirlwind rudely tost,
Through boundless space—be driven—scatter'd—lost !

NOTE.—The incident mentioned in these lines occurred after a
violent storm off the rocky coast of one of our English islands. *Wraith's
Bay*, as the common people called it, was by some persons thought to
derive its name from the Saxon word for a ghost or spirit ; it being re-
markable for the number of dead bodies drifting into its wild receptacle
after shipwrecks, which once were frequent on that treacherous coast.

O WORLD! NOW MY BIRTHPLACE.

O WORLD! now my birthplace, when soon I must
    leave thee,
  What region shall offer the outcast a home?
Will my spirit rejoice to be changeless and free?—
  Midst clusters of stars be permitted to roam?

O'er the spots that it loved shall it pass in a ray
  Of sunshine through halls now forsaken by mirth?—
Shall it sail on a moonbeam to pilot the way
  For lovers to meet in the Edens of Earth?

In those orchards of bloom shall it once more delight,
  Where orchis and lily sit low at the feet
Of the moss-grown old trees, and see deftly alight
  The footsteps of Spring at old Winter's retreat?

When the hyacinth's lip, smiling welcome, hath curl'd,
  Fresh flowers their banks and their valleys have found,
When mysterious ferns, their green banners unfurl'd,
  Are waving in woods to the rivulet's sound ;—

Oh, with them would I be ! for sweet Echo breathes still
    The voices of youth that once challenged the air ;
And my heart—though with sadness that Echo might fill—
    Is now vainly longing to thither repair.

If unworthy I'm deem'd of a far greater bliss
    In spheres that we people with all to us dear,
Then to Fortune I pray give enjoyment like this,
    And Pity shall keep her oft-coveted tear !

A DREAM.

D AY'S story told, there comes a stranger tale :
　　The inner life's strong wrestling in our sleep ;
How, though untrod the cold sepulchral vale,
　A strange communion with the dead we keep !

*　　*　　*　　*　　*

The hour I knew not, when a sudden sound
　Pierced through the night and on my slumber broke ;
Familiar once, unearthly now, it found
　Some secret echo could the spell invoke,
Here to recall what melody had been
　In other scenes, and in the days gone by
When night and day were both alike serene,
　With youthful choirs chanting Time's lullaby.

To hear that voice again I lent mine ear :
　It was not Fancy that my sense misled,
The risen North wind's blast I could not hear
　Driving the sear leaves to their autumn bed.
I look'd around, where shone the taper's gleam
　Athwart the Crucifix upon the wall,

G

There yet was time, ere morn, to haply dream
  And fond illusions once more to recall.
In alter'd mood now Night withdraws her veil,
  And spectral hosts rise in the vacant frame,
O'er the unknown the recognized prevail,
  But as we knew them they are not the same.

Far distant ages ! dimly shadow'd life,
  As seen in Egypt's tombs beside the Nile,
Stalk forth, defying cold Oblivion's strife,
  In forms colossal—like the sacred pile
Above the desert poised in mystic strength—
  When midnight points unto the polar star [1]
From its deep portal's dark and devious length,
  All whispering things our ken surpassing far.

Now, round an altar slowly pacing by,
  Robed priests chant pæans to the crescent moon,
Then, a fair queen who on a throne doth lie,
  Glides down a river at the golden noon ;
Anon, a flame bursts forth beside tall tow'rs,
  It lights the city, and it burns the ground,
While wandering meteors fall in clustering show'rs,
  Till all has vanish'd with live thunder's sound.

*   *   *   *   *

[1] "The Great Pyramid was so planned as to have its chief passages
looking directly to the quarter of the Pleiades and to the Pole Star at
the latitude it then occupied, in the year 2170 B.C."—*Vide* "*The
Pyramid and the Bible,*" *by a Clergyman, with Introductory Note by
Piazzi Smyth, Astronomer Royal for Scotland.*

Last, in the zenith I hear music's strains
   Floating o'er wafted rainbows in the air ;
The bird of eve some note of these retains,
   Giv'n back when stars unto their tryst repair.

Then all is dissolved !—as mists, storm-propell'd,
   Leap into sunlight, then in blackness range ;
The worlds of fiction, from my sight expell'd,
   Recede in darkness and with swiftness change.
Sleep's weird romance flies dull approaching care.
   From sheltering precinct of the convent near,
Ere yet the matin-bell invite to prayer,
   I hear the cry of waking chanticleer !

THE COMET OF 1864.

MYSTERIOUS stranger in the vault of Heaven !
Thy purpose say, and what the mandate given ?
Where didst thou kindle thy gigantic flame ?
Before the throne of Him of holiest Name ?
Or in the flood that burns with quenchless fire
Wherein the guilty would, in vain, expire ?
An unconsumed and e'er replenish'd pyre !
Thy torch is not the soft and guiding light
That shone o'er Bethlem in that sacred night
When by their flocks the shepherds vigil kept,
And angels' accents through the ether swept.
O'er the air-wave, for ever raised by sound,
Those words are passing, by no limit bound,
The cry vibrates yet that once rent the air,
When Faith had yielded almost to Despair ;
And Earth, in darkness veil'd, refused to see
The Hallow'd Victim dying on the tree !

Hath Earth forgot her Saviour ? and her crime
Steeped in the Lethe of a vicious time ?

Shalt thou arouse her with some fearful shock?
Let sage, astronomer, gainsay and mock:
What boots their lore, bright traveller on high!
Is hell more distant, and is heaven more nigh?
We yearn to know what they must fail to tell:
Our destined end,—and where the spirits dwell.

How vain the utmost that the world can give
To gladden life, and make us joy to live!
What then remains?—can science thus allay
The fears and pangs that cross us on our way?
The blatant triumph of successful skill,
Probing the elements at man's proud will—
How doth it jar upon the listening ear
That, in the calm, the "still small Voice" would hear.

O! muse with Night, in silence sad. *Then* gleam
The "many mansions" which are not a dream!
We see the clouds o'er half th' horizon riven,
We feel the answer, and our doubts forgiven!
And thou, majestic in thy mystic flight,
Whate'er thy mission, or thy aim, thy might,
Thou dost obey!—Hail! then: thy Lord is ours:
He numbers thine, as these our mortal hours.

*　　　*　　　*　　　*　　　*

But speculation's past, and thou art fled!
How many groups of years shall then have sped
O'er our forgotten graves, ere a new race
May greet thee once more in thy orbit's place!

Ere then, what secrets may become reveal'd—
The wondrous Book, at length, with awe unseal'd?
The trumpet-blast, borne on each answering wind,
Has left no dust of trembling man behind ;
But summon'd from the shelter of the tomb
Its early, latest inmate to his doom !

THE MOWER.

H ARK ! 'tis the music of morn and of May,
    The mower is whetting his scythe ;
His minstrel all free at the dawn of the day,
    Mounts heavenward, jocund and blithe ;

Down on the mead lie the dews of the night,
  As sparkle the gems of Cathay,—
And softly the vapours pass from the sight,
  Like dreams chased by sunbeams away.

Hark ! 'tis the flight of the bee that I hear,
  In secret array'd with her sting :
She hies whither thyme and heather appear—
  But honey alone will she bring?

Bright 'mid the fields are the opening eyes
  Of things that have mourn'd for the sun ;
The flow'rs' meek petals now slowly arise,
  Their course are they once more to run ?

Alas ! that the mower moweth so fast !
  He sharpens the glittering blade—
The lark's ruin'd nest marks where it hath past,
  Dead leaves—all the havoc it made.

Thus better to die than linger till eve,
  The sport of each fickle new hour ;
Storms of the wild, for that garner, we leave
  Where the Mower will cease to have power !

THE EXILE.

WHERE on the margin of the lofty cliff,
    That threatens danger to the passing skiff,
Flora, half-balanced, lays her perfumed hand,
Far from the richer verdure of the land,
While down the steep her chosen gifts she flings,
Light burdens borne to earth on zephyrs' wings.

Where on the strand pale crystals trembling glow,
Kiss'd into radiance by the ebb and flow
Of sportive ripplets dancing to the song
They taught the sisters of the Syren throng—
Where yet more lovely on a summer's night
The shaft of Dian smites the waves with light,
And sends them sparkling, tumbling to the shore
With midnight music never giving o'er.
There was the cradle of his fond romance,
So dazzling still—howe'er the years advance !
Lone in its loveliness—a thought apart--
The Exile's solace, dearest to his heart ;

And dearer now, as midst Life's tangled web
Still shines untarnish'd, one pure golden thread,
Wove in brief space, yet of so rare a strength
It cannot break—unknown as yet its length.
But when the winter of his thoughts comes round,
That zone of light is o'er his mem'ry bound.

THE NYMPH OF AVON.

FAIREST of nymphs! Sweet Avon! would that I
　　Might lay me down awhile all sleepfully,
And in thy wavy folds be borne along
To wake and hear the ocean's nuptial song

Of welcome glad to thee whose cherish'd name
Hath caught the lustre of our Shakespeare's fame;
Soft is thy voice, but it is silent here,
And thou art pensive by a shrine so dear.

Change not thy mood, but mind thee sometimes still
How thou didst rise from earth in humblest rill,
Taking thy way where peaceful harvests stood,
Or, veil'd in twilight, wander'd through the wood.

Now, like a maid who leaves her native vale
To wed a chief o'er whom frowns oft prevail,
Be thine to soothe the Sea-God's chafing-hour,
Bringing thy gentleness in priceless dow'r;

With minstrelsy more sweet than his who charm'd
The Hebrew king when sullen phantoms harm'd—
Thy song resounding o'er the list'ning deep,
In lengthen'd trance the troubled main shall keep.

Sabrina waits—and lowlier bridesmaids meet,
With crystal gifts thy onward steps to greet.
The bridegroom's throne is on the golden wave,—
Thy bower beneath, Love's far-sought gem-lit cave!

Adieu! adieu! I may not see again
This land, o'er which thy bridal course hath lain.
Its storied halls, its castles, fields renown'd—
Pass from me all! and *thou*, the lily-crown'd!

NOTE. The river Avon rises obscurely in the village of Naseby, in
Northamptonshire, not far from the scene of the famous battle, which
occurred in 1645, when the army of King Charles the First was utterly
defeated by the rebel forces under Cromwell and Fairfax. The king
fled to Leicester. The river passes close to the tomb of Shakespeare, at
Stratford-on-Avon, and, after receiving several tributaries, meets the
Severn at Tewkesbury, in Gloucestershire, and they together flow on
peacefully to the ocean. The long and fierce contention of the Houses
of York and Lancaster ended with the battle of Tewkesbury.

AN AFTER-THOUGHT.

A PATH o'erhung with growth of leafy grace,
    That gives with grudging to the footstep space,
High upward leads where woods make pale the light,
Round walls monastic, half-conceal'd from sight.

Scarce heaves its breast the sleeping sea below,
Unless aroused by wave-dividing prow
Of boats advancing from the cavern'd shore,
Impell'd by sail or idly-dipping oar.

Queen of her Bay and Isles in azure sheen,
Parthenope, still spared, surveys the scene
Where once Vesuvius gave to waste the plain,
And human life for refuge fled in vain.

But danger, like the winter's storm, gives place
To hours of peace that peril's worst efface.
The earthquake ceased, the fire's fierce breath grown cold,
Abounding Beauty seeks her ways of old.

Beside this path a rustic bower is found,
With grateful shelter all the seasons round.
'Twas here it fortuned friends unlook'd-for met,
And in these words the younger's thoughts were set :—

Welcome, most welcome, Anselm! is this hour!—
My heart is faint, my head well-nigh o'erwrought
With labour'd science, intricate, and deep.
Have I not kept the watches of the night
In strict observance of the heavenly orbs?
I of *their* destiny may something read :

My own? vainly I dare to penetrate!
Thou, whose aidful staff points to the import
Of the Egyptian's dark yet truthful speech.
Yea, thou the traveller in life's dim eve
Mayst see this athlete's form beside thee here,
Struck like a lion in the changeful chase
Death-doom'd!—with all its strength coil'd up at once,
Whilst thou, the sport of blunted spears, liv'st on,
Scarce thankful for thy painful days prolong'd!

*　　*　　*　　*　　*

What next?—"oblivious Death"—shall this suffice?
Oh, then, despair may blot out life with shame
In very terror of no future bliss!
Shall those we love past utterance of love—
Angels of Earth compelling thoughts of Heav'n—
Shall *these* too cease to be—lost utterly?

All, all, all, cast away like broken gems
To basely mingle with discarded dust ;
Look'd on no more ? It cannot, cannot be !

  Anselm ! I scorn'd thy fane and narrow creeds,
But I am ill at ease. List thou to this :
In dreams I see the judgment throne of Him
Who gave me breath ! *There*, there with fast-clutch'd
    scrolls
Close writ with doubts, emptiness of knowledge,
I hear demoniac laughter, triumph, gibes,
See Angels weep, the gates of Heaven close ;
And He disowns me Whom I did disown.
Then, rise dark shadows round my giddy head,
A sound is in mine ear, a changeless sound,
That syllables *one* word—" Remorse ! Remorse !"

  Yon coral-fisher in Sorrento's Bay
Is happier far than I who can unlock
The secret casket of that dreaded mount,
Lifting its spire of vapour softly now
Through undisturb'd and fragrant matin air,
All known to me its varied elements.
Look ! where the toiler on that tranquil sea,
Catching the sound of prayer-inviting bell,
Lays down his oar and makes that holy sign
I ridiculed as Superstition's trick !

  Father, 'tis true I give—thou sayest so—
At last a thought—an after-thought, to God.
Poor tribute this ! but, Anselm, mark the while

Age points not yet to furrow'd brow, I stand
Revered in schools, nor hath the Tempter ceased
To bring the luscious fruit that lures and slays.
Yet now, methinks, I once did somewhere read
Of peace surpassing all the Stoics give :
Is *this* book found upon thine ancient shelves ?
Thy cell is near, and I will follow thee !

THE CARNIVAL OF NIGHT.

H AIL reign of Dreams! the Carnival of Night!
Dull Day retreats demurely from our sight,
And freights of thought, all gay with ribbon'd mast,
Spread ample sail, and fear no latent blast.

There are fair mansions which we visit oft,
Gardens our own with waving trees aloft,
Roses beloved of birds from Thracian nests,
Appealing nightly to our loving breasts.

Beneath Heav'n's arch the constellations sing,
While Earth's loud plaudits through the welkin ring,
By Orpheus led, with star-encircled lyre [1]—
To strains like these could mortal's art aspire?

[1] The people of Libethrum, in Thrace, claimed the honour of
possessing the burial-place of Orpheus, and farther observed that the
nightingales, which built their nests near his tomb, sang with greater
melody than all other birds. Orpheus is said by some to have received
divine honours after his death, and his lyre to have become one of the
constellations in the heavens.—*See Dr. Smith's Classical Dictionary.*

Behold an Isle with peerless cestus bound
Of changeless blossoms through the seasons round,
Unknown the lands where winter scorns to smile,
And win the sun-beams that might frost beguile.

Safe anchor cast, our trim and gala boat
Rests in the calm where it awhile will float,
With feet unsandall'd, we then press the sand,
Kiss'd by the breeze that perfumed groves hath fann'd,—

The language learn, so eloquent to mock
Sad Ocean's wail within the hollow'd rock,
Where vagrant ripplets storm the helpless cell
Of airy sprites imploring there to dwell.

Fair Mermaids rise, and with alluring call
The sea-ropes [1] weave, that fast our steps enthrall,
Then with their arms 'twined round the halcyon's neck,
Dive deep again to seek a weed-hung wreck.

If winds awake, the Sea-Gods' steeds we drive
Swift o'er the foam-fleck'd race-course of the tide;
Or, e'er they vanish in a land-lock'd bay
And heavenward mount in many-tinted spray,

---

[1] *Chorda filum.* In England it is often called *sea-laces*; in Orkney, *catgut*; in Shetland, *Lucky Minny's lines*; in Ayrshire, *dead men's ropes*. It has been known to cause death when bathing, by the body becoming entangled with it. This singular growth represents the round-reins of carriage-harness, and affords sport to children "playing at horses," etc.—*See Phyc. Brit.* Pl. cvii. and *Popular Hist. of Seaweeds,* by Landsborough.

We skim the stream, or down the valley range ;
New scenes arise, and rapid is the change.
Now, forms beloved with happy smiles appear
And gently ask : " Why shed the useless tear?

" Come, walk with us upon the mountain-side,
And count the stars as o'er its crest they glide.
The eaglet's eye is dim compared with ours
That see the Peris in those brilliant bowers ! "

  *   *   *   *

What brief content, reality to deem
This merry masque, and parting but the dream !
Would that such visions only past away ;
Nor cold experience found as false by day !

Oh ! then when Cereus sets her petals free,
Whisp'ring soft accents of their transient glee
To night-flowers weeping o'er their early doom
Of evanescence, and of pallid bloom,

Forth from the melting rainbow of the moon
Descend, sweet Phantasy ! with this thy boon ;
No 'larum fear, nor heed the long-drawn sigh
Of day's exhaustion, for thy triumph's nigh !

ELEGY ON A MIGRATORY BIRD.[1]

ONE hour ago, sweet pilgrim bird,
 Thy voice from midst the flowers rose ;
Those plaintive notes no more are heard,
 And shades of death around thee close.

Thy wing must cease to speed its flight,
 With aim to find the distant nest ;
No sunny morn shall chase the night,
 And fill with joy thy gentle breast.

We know not what thy tale may be—
 If thou art gone to meet thy mate,
Or ling'ring here she looks for thee,
 Unthinking she is desolate.

Within my hand thy form I lay
 Poor victim of unequal strife !
How little stole thy breath away,
 But who can give thee back thy life ?

[1] Picked up just as the writer was leaving a friend's house in the country.

Then rest beneath fair Holmwood's bow'rs :
    The evening-wind shall yield its sigh,
And roses mourn in leafy show'rs
    When all of summer passeth by.

Perchance that *thou* mayst aid to keep
    Some thought of me with long-loved friends,
When I am gone, like thee, to sleep
    Where life's last fitful wand'ring ends.

NOTE.—The reader may remember the pathetic narrative in Gessner's "Tod Abel's," where Death is first made known to Eve in a dead bird. On hearing the plaintive cry, and seeing the agitation of a bird flying in little circles round and round, and then with ruffled feathers helplessly perching itself on some low branches, Eve draws nearer and beholds another bird laid lifeless on the grass before the mourner. She contemplates it a long while, then lifts it up and endeavours to awaken it. "It wakes not," she says, and with trembling hand lays it down. "It will never awake!" She weeps. Addressing the other, she continues, "That which thou mournest, perhaps, ah! perhaps was thy mate!" In her anguish Eve exclaims—"Ich bin's, die Fluch und Elend über die Erde, über jedes Geschöpfe gebracht hat, du unschuldig Leidender, ich bin's, ich Elende! . . . [Gessner—*Der Tod Abel's*, Zweiter Gesang.]

FLEURS-DE-LIS.

ROYAL lilies of the stream !
　　Tall and queenly as ye seem,
Would ye not forego your state
　　To essay another fate ?

Varied scenes may have their charms,
　　Even when the trial harms ;
See the world, then know ye first
　　What it is for rest to thirst.

Comes no cross, ye cannot tell
   Good the home where now ye dwell ;
Contrast rude, though hard to meet,
   Fortune's smile makes doubly sweet.

Would ye not the swallow's wing,
   Or such light and harmless thing,
Swept a moment o'er your calm,
   If 'twere but a brief alarm ?

Would ye not th' impartial wind
   Search'd the leaves that round you bind,
And your heads in meeker guise
   Bent a moment from the skies?

Change ye with Arabia's flowers,
   Where the desert's heat devours
Dew-drops burnt by cruel morn,
   And for company the thorn !

Crush'd, maybe, 'neath camel's hoof,
   Ah ! ye need no further proof
Pleasant now your lives to deem
   Royal lilies ! by your stream.

A voice I hear ! it seems to say
   " Thoughtless are thy words this day !"
Pardon flowers, fair and sad !
   Memory is seldom glad.

Noble was your fame acquired
   When King Philip, " The Desired,"
Sought to plant you in his shield,[1]
   Bidding foemen to you yield.

Ancestry of such far date,
   Where now all is desolate,
Fortune won and too soon lost,
   Yea ! ye *have* been tempest-tost !

It is past—then best forget
   Palaces where once ye met ;
Harp and lute are tuneless now,
   Sorrow on your Prince's brow ;

Silence broods within his hall,[2]
   Rare the sound of footstep's fall ;
In the forest, in the glade,
   Solitude her home hath made.

---

[1] Philippe Auguste, A.D. 1180-1223. " La figure de son contre-scel qui m'a esté communiquée par M. Justel, Secrétaire du Roi, et c'est le *plus vieux monument que j'aye pû trouver, où il paroisse de Fleur-de-Lys.*"—*Abrégé, etc., Histoire de France*, par M. de Brianville, 1675.

[2] The Château de Chambord (at some distance from Blois), which was the Versailles of Touraine, until it was deserted by Louis XIV. for the palace nearer Paris. It was in this grand but gloomy Château that Francis I. wrote—in the presence of his sister " La Marguerite des Marguerites " (The Pearl of Margarets), who vainly endeavoured to dispel the depression of his spirits the well-known lines :—

      " *Souvent femme varie*
     Mal habil qui s'y fie."

        [*See " Histoire de Blois,*" par Bernier.]

Round the chapel drear and lone,
　Live your emblems carved in stone ;
Still the priest holds firm belief,
　Prayers may yet restore his chief.

Monarch of a small domain,
　Subjects there are his in vain,
Where the Exile's only boast
　Echoes from a phantom host.

Happier ye! from out the woods
　Courtiers come in winning moods :
Flying to you through the air,
　Solemn[1] now—now debonnair,

Welcome is that warbling throng
　Matin-call and evensong,
And ye'll hear the river tell
　Tales of where its people dwell.

[1] "With this her solemn bird."—MILTON.

K

ACROSS THE DEEP.

WHEN in the age of eager youth
    The pilgrim's staff he sought,
How hasted he to test the truth
    Of tales the old man taught.

His feet were bound in sandal-shoon,
   His flask hung by his side ;
All but the scallop-shell, that soon
   He'd win across the tide.

But on the way he loiter'd long,
   And view'd the world's rich mart,
Bartering, like the giddy throng,
   With precious time to part.

Forgotten was the unseen shrine,
   The pilgrim's garb thrown off ;
Young cavaliers so brave and fine
   His former mood might scoff.

One morn a cry dispell'd his sleep,
   He hasten'd to the shore,
His friends had pass'd across the deep,
   And would return no more.

And not till then, the anchor lost,
   The ship's due course was run—
He knew full well at what a cost
   The pilgrim's shell is won.

TO ———

THERE may be bards who win the laurel crown
 In fields Elysian, while all mildly melt
The days away, far from misfortune's frown,
 And safe from shocks the world to others dealt.

But o'er *my* harp no touch of seraph's wing,
 Melodious passing, woke th' inspirèd lay :
Dark angels struck, and still discordant ring
 The long vibrations where they took their way.

And though my song be once more glad again
 With all that Poesy might there evoke,
Not free from sadness is the later strain,
 And 'midst the chords the tunefullest is broke.

Alas ! you would not that my verse reveal'd
 The fatal truths that thrill the aching heart ;
And yet those truths, though for a time conceal'd,
 Who can dismiss, and wholly keep apart ?

Who may escape the fate that life entails ?
 Who dare corruption to attack his prey ?
Nor earth's nor ocean's deepest cave avails
 To hide the victim, or the robber stay !

In vain ideal Fancy strives to fan
  The flame which should illume all mortal things :
In bird, in flow'r, and most in godlike man,
  Behold the ruin Death's dark presence brings !

The torch reversed—can eye pierce through the night
  To which no day-spring is vouchsafed us here ?
Religion's rapture and her faith's strong might
  Exhausted droop before the silent bier.

Is there forgiveness for such failing strength ?
  Grief's midnight cloud obscures the path to Heav'n :
But when the stars undimm'd shine forth at length,
  The sign of Pardon in the Cross is giv'n.

NOTE.

" Io mi volsi a man destra, e posi mente
All' altra pole, e vidi quattro stelle
Non viste mai fuor ch'alla prima gente."

DANTE, *Il Purgatorrio.*

" . . . As sea voyages round the Cape of Good Hope and in the Pacific Ocean . . . multiplied, and as Christian missionaries pressed forward into the newly discovered lands of America, the fame of this constellation increased more and more. The first Spanish settlers in tropical America were accustomed to infer the hour of the night from the inclined or perpendicular position of the Southern Cross, as is still done. . . . . The earlier inhabitants of our high Northern latitudes might see this magnificent Southern constellation rise to their view—which will not now reappear for thousands of years. It began to be invisible in 52½° N. latitude 2,900 years B.C., when it vanished from the horizon to countries adjoining the Baltic. The great Pyramid of Cheops had already been standing in Egypt for five centuries. The pastoral nation of the Hyksos made their invasion 700 years later, *i.e.* 1,200 years before Homer, 2,200 of our era.—*Vide Humboldt's Cosmos, trans. by Sabine,* vol. ii. pages 123, 208, 209.

IN MEMORY OF THE HON. J. A.

THE land of song is now his rest
    Who early from our midst departs,
Yet, living and to memory prest—
    A silent image in our hearts.

No rayless vault its couch may lend,
    He sleeps beneath a cloudless sky,
And o'er his head the wild flow'rs bend
    Responsive to the soft wind's sigh.

What harmony comes down from heaven
    In those all matchless southern nights!
A lullaby for moonbeams given,
    Impeding their too wayward flights :

The Saint[1] of Music's sweetest strain,
  Low sweeping through cathedral aisle,
To match the sea-chants were in vain,
  That night and day the hours beguile.

Along the shore, beneath the tomb,
  Sequester'd on the neighb'ring hill,
In deep repose, but not in gloom,
  A holy requiem sounding still.

The resurrection of the morn,
  The glory of the wakening scene,
Prophetic of a life new-born,
  A brighter than the past hath been.

[1] Saint Cecilia.

TO ——

T AKE back thy flow'r ! Give not to me
    An emblem of decay ;
I would not have, and least from *thee*,
    A thing that fades away :

One ray.too fierce, a gust too keen
    Will shake it from its throne—
A lovely and a smiling queen,
    In halcyon days alone !

But rather steal from yonder rock
    The golden lichen's leaf—
For it hath borne each season's shock
    (Ah ! summer-time is brief !)—

And o'er that riven stone hath flung
    A soft and living hue,
Like pity, when from sternness wrung
    By mournful tale and true ;

Thus mingling with an adverse fate,
    A faith that will not change—
Unfaltering, if ne'er abate
    The storms within its range.

Though quaint the token, be it mine !
    Nay !—smile not at my choice :
It tells of constancy like thine,
    "Twill bid my heart rejoice.

Withhold thy gentle hand, nor lay
    Frail flowers down in mine—
Would'st thou foretell a coming day
    When love too must decline ?

I.

FAREWELL TO EARTH.

FAREWELL to Earth! the world adieu!
　　For breath I would disdain to sue ;—
And since we must for ever part,
No sigh shall tell a failing heart,
Nor dim the eye, nor dull the ear
Death's herald stern to see and hear.
But quick as youth's undrowsy life
When for the mortal combat rife ;—
Yea ! 'tis best that we should sever—
Grief with age encounter never !
'Tis but a worthless world at best,
For years of toil a moment's rest ;
For one hope blest, a thousand crush'd ;
Ambition that our boyhood flush'd,
Wither'd and blasted like the pine
Whose lofty height must first decline,
That shoots to heav'n, and dares alike
The light to bless—or flash to strike !
Long years outlive their very life,
The limbs are with the soul at strife.

And pain and suff'ring wear away
The sense of joy—cloud reason's ray,
And leave man helpless, useless, weak,
And peevish folly there will seek
To level wisdom in her eld
With all that childhood's morn beheld !

And thus is age ;—and youth, hope fools
With dreams that stern experience schools.
The jocund hours how soon they pass !
And griefs in frequency surpass—
In keenness too, joy's utmost thrill ;
And chequer'd life is changing still !
Ay ! youth is trusting, thoughtless, fond,—
Nor looks the present hour beyond—
Then wakes too late, and starts to feel
How much can cold deceit reveal !
To writhe beneath the galling pain
Of passions, fruitless, hapless, vain !—
To see, to hear, the syren Bliss,
But beckon o'er despair's abyss.
Oh, why prolong life's weary lease
Nor gladden at the soul's release ?—
Death shall not wrest a tear from one
Who glories that his race is run !—
Then friends and foes alike, adieu !
Feign not a sorrow strange to you ;
'Tis mockery to act the part
That must belie your reckless heart ;
Forget as ye'll be soon forgot—
Such fate wing'd years to most allot.

A gentler word to warmer breasts,
With them my parting blessing rests,
Would it could bring them more than joys
That lighten as Time's bolt destroys;—
Would it could spare from ills of earth !
Alas ! they haunt man from his birth,
And crown his baby head with thorns
That pierce the deeper as life dawns !
Yet—ye who love me take the all
My heart can yield—the spoil though small
Once fill'd a mine of feelings deep,
Where Passion did her empire keep ;
Affections moulded not to suit
Perchance the world, and therefore mute ;
The love of kindred minds, but not
The giddy gay in fashion's knot ;—
The midnight dense, the idle hour
That on the mind must lead or sour, ···
These never could my thoughts enthrall,
But vanish'd swift at Nature's call.

The boundless heath, the tawny burn,
The dell o'erfleck'd with tufts of fern—
The cowslip bank, the breezy down,
To stand upon its sunlit crown
And snuff the air like mettled steed
That pants to try his utmost speed ;
To sweep th' horizon with an eye
Whose light seem'd then could never die ;
To clasp a gentle hand, and think
Time's pathway never near'd a brink,—

Oh, these were joys could never tire,
I might no other gifts require :—
A heart below, a God above—
For more would man or live or love?

NEW YEAR'S EVE.

THE rousing chimes that bid the waning Night
    Go forth to meet the advent of the Year,
Have lost their spell or are not tuned aright,—
    Methinks it is a passing bell I hear.

A tried, though not all-faithful, friend retires—
    His fickle mood, the form, the smile, we knew :
There comes a stranger round our household fires,
    Without remembrance, and with aspect new.

What doth he bring ?   Forbear to question him :—
    Look on bright glory's semblance in the cloud,
Its shape of beauty and its golden rim,
    Nor think the while it is a chilling shroud !

Alas ! my thoughts mount upward to life's spring,
    Where play'd its bubbles on the mountain air,
Or else they drift in vain imagining,
    To seek the future in its dreaded lair !

SPIRITS OF THE DEAD.

SPIRITS of the Dead!—be ye what ye may,
    Let not conjecture guide our thoughts astray ;
With claspèd hands we breathe the prayers of Earth—
If ye be free, give knowledge to our dearth :
In night so fair, come o'er the mead of stars,
And with their rays pass through our prison-bars.

Teach us, in utterance your own, to sing
Like cagèd bird his freed mate answering :
When all but this is hush'd with hidden day
He hears her voice where, on the lofty spray
Of aspen trembling in the distant grove,
She tells her sorrow and her deathless love ;
And as she sings—sings ere the day be past,
He comes all joyfully, released at last !

O Spirits of the loved and lost ! now blest,
Soothe us till eve with you bring tardy rest !
Or, from incomparable joy above,
Send, if ye will, the welcome herald-dove,
Her message closed within some emblem-flow'r,
That only blooms beneath a seraph's bow'r.

MORNING IN PROVENCE.

THE air scarce lifts the aspen-leaf,
    Or sheds the grain from bending sheaf,
Helps not to drift the fairy rope
Where poor Arachne set her hope :
The wandering lightest feather'd seed
Floats on its way with stinted speed.

Come then, my harp! we'll sing the hours,
As forth they come from Eastern tow'rs—
    Clad in vesture pearly grey
    Ere the night be mourn'd away—
Kindling a thousand dewdrop fires—
Soft light that all too soon expires!

How gently morn around them flings
The golden robe Apollo brings,—
And o'er their brow blush-roses wreathes,
With perfumes that the violet breathes—
A lovely group of heavenly birth
Advancing o'er the wakening Earth!

Still on the sea, like sapphire set
'Mid classic lands—there linger yet
Departing shadows of the night
Though distant Esterel's peaks are bright.

The moorland tarn in mossy cell,
By lonely bittern known so well,
Enshrines within its calm lagoon
The beam of sun or midnight moon.
With not more clear and tranquil rest
Than at this hour—of all the best—
Doth Napoule's deep and slumb'ring bay
Reflect the star of coming day,
Beside the dusky mountain's feet,
Where olive groves with cypress meet.

M

Is there no harp, but only mine,
Attuned to sing of scenes like thine,
Sweet Provençe ?—*where* thy troubadour,
Or knight enamour'd on gay tour—
Swift hast'ning hither o'er the plain
To serenade fair Châtelaine?
Thy minstrel bards—oh, where are they ?
Let them take up my skill-less lay,
And sing of these bewitching hours
In some old castle's myrtle bow'rs !

For eventide suits me the best—
Till then my harp and I will rest ;
We'll saunter where the lilies' gleam
Shall tempt to muse along the stream,
Beneath the crags where changeless snow
Forbids to know a warmer glow,
And heark'ning there may haply hear
The fabled swan enchant the ear.

RELICS OF THE PAST.

I 'VE taken from the old oak chest
  The relics of the past,
There garner'd when the hours were blest,
  And cherish'd to the last !

The thoughts, the vows of other days,
  Traced by the well-known hand,
Speak, while the dimm'd eye o'er them strays,
  As from a distant land.

Some have to grating discord turn'd
 The music of their sound;
The harmony to some return'd,—
 But *one* was changeless found.

The faded flowers I gently lift
 From whence conceal'd they lay :
Alas ! the giver and the gift
 Alike have pass'd away.

I open last of all the shrine
 Where life seems ling'ring still !—
One treasure left that yet is mine,
 On which Time works no ill !—

In beauty's hue, the test withstood,
 Death's touch it seems to mock :
Bright as when we, in joyous mood,
 Exchanged the sever'd lock !

Back to your cell ! each hallow'd charm,
 From colder eyes apart,
And hid from hands that might you harm,
 Sweet captives of my heart !

Thrice hallow'd now, for evermore,
 O relics of the past !
Where the dark Angel passing o'er,
 His fatal shadow cast !

AUTUMN LEAVES.

A S lonely and sad I watched Autumn's rich glory,
    Scatter'd in leaves that fell thickly around me,
I heard their low voices thus whisper the story :
    "Oh, ever Life's visions were thus unto thee!

" In the Spring-time's fresh morning we burst on the light,
    While fann'd by the softest of zephyr's warm breath,
And fair Summer beheld how our beauty was bright,
    Though Ruin was tracking her victims by stealth.

" There is gold in our hue, as though yet the sun shone,
    But 'tis not the radiance of youth's happy day ;
And full soon with the rest 'twill deceive, and be gone
    To perish and fade in the shade of decay.

" Oft the insect, in search of our life-juice, that sips,
    Will steal the rich hue of our garment the while;
And stern Death in the rainbow his shaft sometimes dips—
    Ere darkly he strikes—thy fond hope to beguile.

" Thy last years are fallen now stricken by sorrow,
    The star of their ev'ning is hopelessly fled ;
Thy smile is akin to the tints that we borrow,
    Concealing the heart that is dying or dead !

" But how wide is thy destiny parted from ours!—
    The spoil of mortality but for a time :
We perish for ever, 'neath Winter's cold showers—
    Thou but diest to live in heaven's own clime !"

LIFE IN DREAMS.

" Si fué mi maestro un sueño,
Y estoy temiendo en mis ansias,
Que he de dispertar, y hallarme
Otra vez en mi cerrada
Prision ; y cuando no sea,
El soñarlo solo basta." . . .

CALDERON—*La Vida es sueño.*

L OVED home of my youth ! Fare thee well then
    for ever !
All thoughts of thee henceforth belong to the past ;
Though Fate has decreed that at length we must sever,
   Remembrance of thee fondly clings to the last.

In dreams I shall sit by the fount on thy terrace,
   Where myrtle and vine throw soft shadows around,
Or seek the steep path where the riven rocks menace
   To fall 'mid wild forms long since strewn on the ground.

In a dream shall I lie on those crystal-bright sands
   'Neath coppice and knoll daisies claim for their own—
The clarion to hear of those swift-wing'd serried bands
   That guides unto nests in far forests unknown.

Was no meaning discern'd—no presage discover'd—
 I' the wail of the waves - the sudden wind's chill—
When the Dayspring o'er Night so tremblingly hover'd,
 And knew that her promise was hard to fulfil?

Glad scenes of my youth ! Yes, if all else should perish,
 No change can come o'er my devotion to you.
What once I so loved, I must madly still cherish,
 Though cypress and yew marr'd the rose where it grew.

One by one they who loved thee, so early, so late,
 For ever are gone,—only strangers remain ;
And these may neglect thee, while, cold as its climate,
 The land of the Gael they will seek to regain !

GUARDIAN ANGELS

ANGELS so near?—to what fine sense appeals
   The heavenly presence that its form conceals?
Are they encompass'd with celestial might,
Yet soft as shimmer of the Northern Light?
As Love persuasive in Love's stillest hour—
Silent as moonbeams in sequester'd bower?
Bright as the smile that greets the rover home,
With mute entreaty that he cease to roam?

Melodious, too? as lays that waft once more
The sighs of age to youth's deserted shore?
Fragrant as flowers unseen that scent the air,
Leaving our fancy to depict them fair?
Soothing like carol of the distant rill
All hast'ning down the marble font to fill—
Leaping and falling there in cadence meet,
With drops like gems dissolving at our feet?

       *   *   *   *   *

Ah! what avail comparisons like these?—
On heav'nly theme can mortal's language please?

NEW YEAR'S BELLS.

YE New Year's bells! Ye Old Year's bells!
　　What gossip now your jangle tells?
Swinging, ringing, "farewell" giving—
　　Ringing, swinging, "welcome" bringing.

Scarce pleases me a double tongue
　　The children of the world among,
When welcome to the newer friends
　　With sadder words at parting blends.

I cared not for thee Olden Year!—
　　Thou wert not worth a sigh or tear:
And yet, when thou and I must part,
　　A shadow finds my careless heart:—

That shadow follows on a word—
　　Oh, lightly never breathed or heard—
And in sorrow often spoken,
　　When some link to life is broken,

Now piercing through the breast that's riv'n
  Like northern blast in summer's heav'n,
Or unremember'd winter's frost
  That dooms the May-buds to be lost.

Too powerful in all its meaning,
  Yet too weak to tell our feeling,
That word, "Farewell!" we read in eyes
  Whose eloquence in silence lies. . . .

Away sad thoughts! no more o'erleap
  The boundaries we charged you keep;
Earth's restless flames are hid below
  The surface where the green leaves grow.

Ah! now, methinks, my young crown'd Year,
  Thy cap with bells thou wearest here—
A-fooling with thy pranks and jest;
  Yet hearken to my high behest:

I prythee that thy moons preside
  O'er nights wherein no dangers hide—
Thy sun irradiate coming days,
  And check our fickle climate's ways.

Bid Time exact what all must pay—
  His tribute—in a courteous way:
A gentle conqueror, whose pow'r
  Oppresses not the passing hour.

Then, ring thy bells ! thy welcome give
To those who yet may care to live ;
And on eve of life's last morrow,
Accents from the angels borrow.

THE LAST VOYAGE.

HAIL! mortal, hail! Oh, fear not me,
   Nor dread the wind and wave—
My galley on the wildest sea
   Is tranquil as the grave.

I heard thee sigh: " Who with thee went
   Returnèd never more !"
Yet follow me—I'm hither sent
   The parted to restore.

Oh, courage, man ! thy mates rejoice
   To search for unknown lands :
How oft it is their eager choice
   To clasp my outstretch'd hands !

Shall this be at Ambition's nod ?
   Or for the wage of gold ?
At beck of some elected god
   To whom their sense is sold ?

I challenge thee, forsooth ! to fight
　　Against my sovereign power !
I wear no trappings of a knight,
　　But thou shalt surely cower.

Your heroes, chieftains, ye revere
　　Their mandates will obey—
Go ! bring to me their annals here,
　　And point to the array :

Proud of the paltry hosts they slew—
　　Their victories—their fame :
I'll show thee *mine*—spoils old and new !
　　The *dust* from whence they came !

Canst thou count out each sep'rate grain ?
　　Quick that reckoning's done !
A rebel dost thou now remain ?
　　Or is submission won ?

'Tis thine to shape my galley's course
　　To Heaven or to Hell :
Then *thine* be all the dark remorse
　　If Death serve thee not well !

IN IMITATION OF THE RHYME
OF ONE OF THE POEMS
OF JULIUS MOSEN.

Dashing,
  Splashing,
Come the waves !
Rock and seaweed
    Wearing,
    Tearing,
While the white foam
    Hasting,
    Wasting,
Sinks away in ocean caves.

    Prancing,
    Dancing,
Come the steeds—

Tide and tempest
        Facing, .
        Racing,
With their bright crests
        Waving,
        Raving,
Rolling on the briny meads.

        Gushing,
        Rushing,
To the strand—
Shipwreck'd plunder
        Bringing,
        Flinging,
On the billows,
        Sifting,
        Drifting,
Ready for the robber's hand.

        Peaceless,
        Ceaseless,
The rude swell,
Corpse of dead man
        Mocking,
        Rocking,
While the seabird
        Flying,
        Crying,
Screams the sailor's dying knell.

Crossing,
Tossing,
To the sea,
Moaning,
Groaning,
As repentant,
Keeping,
Weeping,
Those who come to life no more.

GOOD-NIGHT.

"GOOD-NIGHT!" How oft in earliest years
   Of long delight and transient tears
We've heard, we've spoke, with fond delay,
The words that closed a merry day.
But as the dial's shade declines
To chasten'd thought the mind inclines :
Oh, then, when anger, anguish, pain,
Refuse that sleep should lull the brain,
Though stilless, all, may court repose,
The watchful eyes refuse to close—
By Mem'ry's lamp still on and on
They bend to read that page whereon
The story of our life we trace—
Could Lethe's stream those lines efface ?

Remember'd tones of happier eld,
We wish prophetic meaning held !—
Thus, pilgrims in the flush of morn
Deem not their strength will e'er be worn—
Nor how at eve with painful sigh
They yet may wish that home were nigh !

Thou ! who, though stricken, yet can rest,
Woe-worn, by slumber's weight opprest,—
Thrice blest to thee the day's decline,
The earnest of repose that's thine.
Eve, 'neath her pale-gemm'd veil, with smile
'Twixt joy and grief, now rests awhile :
Then, as she fades, soft teardrops leaves
Among the reeds and golden sheaves :
Then darkness falls—the banner waves
That stays the fight which noontide braves—
The hostile hosts of Thought retire—
Their watchfires, as they sleep, expire.

There as thou liest, from fearful Death
Distinct but in thy warmth of breath,
What anxious life bestirs within,
The new felicity to win !—
How swift, how eager thence to mount
Guideless and free unto the fount
Where dreams and fancies take their birth
With angel's smile or demon's mirth !—
To mock or soothe in varying guise,
Alternate as those phantoms rise !

In vapours wreathed of dazzling light
Unearthly forms illume thy night ;
Unearthly sounds thy welcome ring,
And not of us are they who sing.
The smile that on thy lip now plays
A happiness unknown betrays ;

That murm'ring soft that meets the ear
None to interpret findeth here.—
Speed ! speed! fast runs the reck'ning sand,
Held in its glass by spectral hand !—
The Hours obey their tyrant, Time,
And wait to rouse thee with their chime. . . . .

Too late ! 'tis o'er—Elysium fades !
Thy wandering in her lovely glades
Must cease as morn with sudden glare
Calls unto thee her task to share.

Oh, who can speak the deep distress
Of waking to life's bitterness?—
That yearning of the troubled mind
Which nevermore its peace shall find?

'Tis Fate's relentless sword of flame
Driving us back from whence we came—
Again unto the desert cast,
The Paradise of Dreams is past.

THOUGHTS BY THE WAY-SIDE.

"La vita fugge, e non s'arresta un' ora;
E la morte vien dietro a gran giornate."--PETRARCA.

H, happy time!
oh, happy
time!
When in sun-
shine dan-
cing,
Wild Hope, with
Childhood
in its prime,
Each joy is
enhancing!

Oh, happy time! Oh, time of bliss!
Youth's rainbow-tinted morn,
When on the brow Love sets his kiss
With roses newly born.

Unseen the clouds that slowly creep
Beneath the horizon's glow;
Unfelt the winds so soon to sweep
And lay the dancers low;—

The pang unknown—the thoughts that come
  In Memory's motley train—
Regret to all, remorse to some—
  How soon our path they gain !

O Time ! thy wings are dark in age,
  Though not less swiftly spread ;
They cast a shadow o'er the page
  Where once we brightly read !

The book of Life—its fitful tale—
  How will the story end ?
Christ ! let the prayer at length prevail,
  And angels o'er it bend :—

The songs of early Hope and Love,
  Let them be heard again !
And sung by those who sing above
  The pure immortal strain !

IN THE OLDEN TIME.

SAINT BERNARD in the town of Spire
    Had stirr'd its men with sacred fire,
And to the holiest shrine on earth
Sent pilgrims arm'd of gentle birth.

That saint revered, by Dante seen
In Paradise with glory's sheen,
Of Clairvaux famed, and still held dear
When to his hospice we draw near.

Among the knights that bid for fame
Came one of lordly Brœmser's name,
And heir was he to a domain
Renown'd in reign of Charlemagne,—

When Rüdesheim, to vintage known,
Preferr'd a nobler claim to own,
And held that court in Ingelheim,
We read of, in the olden time.

Conrad his watch-of-arms had kept,
But there was one, meantime, who wept—
Fair Ermingarde, betroth'd of late
To him who leaves her desolate!

For warriors' hearts, though cased in steel,
The wound of Beauty's glances feel;
And thus the youth by Beauty's sight
Was vanquish'd once—but not in fight.

Then by her gentle self he swore
To love with truth for evermore—
An oath that death alone could break—
If perjured, Fate revenge would take.

The Lover's Oath.

I swear not by the jewels set
  Round Heaven's crown, however bright—
In daylight we those gems forget,
  And they are gifts of sable night!

Nor care I by the fiery sun
  To pledge my word of honest truth—
In darkness half his course is run,
  Ill-omen'd oath might lead to ruth.

The feeble moon I swear not by,
  When she sails wand'ring on her way—
Who heeds the vow or vapid sigh
  Of lovers fickle as her sway?

By that which will not change, I'll swear—
  Thy Soul—that burns like vestal's flame,
Unmoved by breath of earthly air,
  And pure as when from Heaven it came!

THE WHIRLPOOL AND THE BOAT.

O BOATMEN, row !—oh, row like men
　　Who row for life
　　Or wager's strife
And idle strokes condemn !

　The stream runs fast, and this ye feel
　　As now the tide
　　With eager pride
Uplifts the buoyant keel.

Our galley flies like swallow's wing,
　　To skim the wave,
　　And danger brave,
And homeward us to bring.

On ! on ! against the rising wind !—
　　Nor rest an oar
　　Until Saint Goar
Ye leave a league behind !

And when the Mountains Seven appear,
　　Cheer, cheer ye then
　　Like merry men,
For rest from toil is near.

My bugle's note shall then be heard
　　By lady-love
　　Who sits above
Sad singing to her bird.

　　*　　　　*　　　　*　　　　*

Right well each man his duty knew,—
　　But in the night
　　The whirlpool's might
O'erwhelm'd the hapless crew.

HOURS ON THE RHINE.

'TWAS in the month to Mary vow'd—
　　Vow'd by the Church of Rome,—
And on a morn without a cloud
　　Beneath the welkin's dome,

When up the Rhine, too swiftly borne,
    Five travellers went by
The fort, with age and battle worn,
    That doth near Cologne lie.

There were of these two men of note,
    The third a student grave—
His brother, one who sketch'd or wrote
    Or thoughts to musing gave ;

Late, from Bellona's tents he came
　　Enamour'd of the arts
That gave to Italy that fame
　　From which she never parts ;—

But he was destined soon to die
　　On Adriatic shore ;
Nor did his youthful look belie
　　The sadness that it wore. . . .

One more I name, to make the five—
　　A gentle, noble dame :
Content seem'd ever best to thrive
　　Where'er her presence came.

With many a legend of folk-lore,
　　These friends beguiled the time,
As each in turn gave up his store
　　Of either prose or rhyme.

Yet, England's bard alone could give
　　That charm which is the Rhine's,
And bid its beauty ever live
　　With music in his lines.

Ah ! who may hope, such harp to hear
　　Along the Pilgrim's way,
Can later poets win that ear
　　Once heark'ning to its lay ?

They pass'd the isle where convent walls
　　Lie on the water's breast,
Beneath the mount whose name recalls
　　The fearful dragon's nest.

Fair Coblentz gave one night to sleep,
　　Then, rising with the day,
They stood upon th' embattled steep,
　　As roll'd the mists away.

Far, far below, on lofty spire,
    The wind-submissive vane
Shone like a lance with point of fire
    Bright glitt'ring o'er the plain.

Where Moselle brings her tribute near
    The everlasting hills,
The toils of commerce re-appear
    In tasks the day fulfils.

Yet there, as ever, sunset's hour
    Must seem the best to muse
O'er ruin'd hopes, o'er shatter'd power,
    And dreams that years diffuse.

Upon the vessel's deck again,
    So rapid was the speed,
That he who sought a sketch to gain
    But mark'd each scene recede.

As thus his useless pencil fell
    All idly from his hand,
The whistled pastorelle might tell
    His thoughts forsook this land.

And like the Tyrolean strain,
    Dear to the mountaineer,

That ditty sung, still o'er again,
   Brought some loved object near.

Yet held these lovely banks their sway
   Congenial to his mind;
Harmonious Ruin's mild decay
   With youth of Spring combined.

Q

How welcome there the spot to trace
  Where foemen cross'd their swords,
And Chivalry with Love kept pace,
  While minstrels struck the chords.

Anon appear'd an antique pile—
  The Pfalz—amidst the stream :
A prison and a fort somewhile,
  Where freedom was a dream.

Less frequent then the rocks arose,
  The hills at length withdrew,
And Nature hush'd seem'd to repose,
  As smiling there anew

In purple shadow's dark'ning hue
  Are stately buildings near,
Above the flood and fair to view
  The cupolas appear.

So smoothly lies that silvery glass
  Within the twilight set,
The wild birds seem, that o'er it pass,
  Beneath by others met.

The Western Star is yet too faint
  Her image there to seek ;
She mounts the sky like chosen Saint,
  Demurely staid and meek.

'Tis Mayence ; and they come to land,
   The pleasant voyage done ;
What fate awaits the little band,
   Shall they part one by one ?

We never bring a happy day
   Unto its final end,
We cannot mark the parting ray
   Beneath the sea descend,

So glorious in its last Farewell!
 Instilling soft regret,
But on some boding thought we dwell :—
 " For ever are they set."

Shall they pass still link'd together
 Adown the stream of life,
Daring sports of fickle weather?
 Heeding not its wayward strife?

What moves the soul with passion's force
 To grasp at worlds unseen?—
Was there a period in its course
 More blest than this hath been,[1]

Leaving some vague remembrance ours,
 Now hovering o'er the mind,
Like downy messengers from flowers,
 A fitting home to find?—

 * * * * *
 * * * * *

The Rhine flows on ! its busy hives
 Cease not to toil and live,
Beauty, that loves the wild, survives
 Her constant charm to give.

---

[1] . . . . . . " The longing for a lost ideal as if in the human breast a degree of melancholy was ever blended with the deeper feelings which the view of nature inspires."—*Cosmos*, vol. ii. p. 12. *See* also *Sakoontali*, vol. ii. p. 12, transl. by Monier Williams.

But where are they of whom I spake,
  That journey'd at sweet will?
What region new of stream or lake
  Finds them united still?

They are gone! those wanderers all!
  No new May-morn to greet,
They answer give to Death's roll-call,
  His legions with them meet.

THE DYING MISSIONARY.

. . . ." a questo regno
Non sali mai, chi non credette in Christo,
Vel pria, vel poi, che si chiavasse al legno."
DANTE. *Paradiso, Canto decimonono.*

I HEAR the voice of Eternal Spring,
   And with harps her Chorus is singing,
I feel the soft air waved by her wing,
   Through the palm-leaves its freshness bringing.

Lay me down on the sand—on the sand,
   Though with fiery heat it is glowing.
Mine eyes but behold the pasture-land
   Where rivers for ever are flowing.

A Hand that was pierced is on my brow,
   And its fever'd furrows there smoothing,
The agony, all, I suffer now,
   The joy at my heart still is soothing.

None, none are near of the faithful few,
   Alone on my tomb I am lying;
Oh, welcome to me Death's hallow'd dew:
   Christ! for Thee am I dying—dying.

NOTE.—St. Francis Xavier died—unattended and alone on the little
island of Sancia—in an attempt to reach China.

THE WELL OF EHRENBREITSTEIN.

BEHOLD a wealth of waters near
　　The mountain-gorge and plain delight !
Sharp pangs of thirst who dreams to fear
　　With noble streams [1] like these in sight ?

But let the foe surround this rock,
　　Whose fortress warriors' arms defend.
Those rivers but the thirsty mock—
　　For who unto their brink may send ?

[1] The Rhine and the Moselle.

Thus Nature with prophetic thought
　The tears of healing pity wept,
And not in vain her sons have sought
　The chalice where those tears are kept.

The shaft struck deep, and in the heart
　Of this bright stone of honour [1] lay
Each previous drop long set apart
　Against the battle's fiery day.

See o'er yon rockly ledge, where lean
　In listless groups full-weary men,
With wistful, watchful eyes and keen,
　That ask shall freedom come, and when?

A doubtful time 'tis theirs to wait,
　Ere they may see the glad release;
For they are prisoners of state,
　Albeit kings may be at peace.

O Freedom! when we live with thee,
　Thou givest life its sweetest zest.
We know not what that gloom may be
　When no more of thy light possest.

But, captives, from whatever wrong,
　The mind will think it loves thee now
Far more than when unbroken song
　Led on the hours—their chantress—*Thou!*

---

[1] Ehrenbreitstein. *Anglice*, broad stone of honour.

SONNET I.

A S from the summit of a tree decay'd
  The feather'd Laureate of triumphal Spring,
His homage in sweet strains delights to sing
By the past lightning's riot undismay'd,

So the bright spirit in its flight delay'd,
  Still to the frailest tenement will cling,
  Some cheering tribute of its own to bring,
Or music stolen, once by zephyr play'd.

O'er the dull path that's haunted by our foe,
  We lighten some slight measure of our pain,
If, like gay scholar, whistling as we go.

When years have fled, and fewer joys remain,
Search thou the leafless banks of Time—we know
  A lingering flower may not be sought in vain!

SONNET 2.

WHEN sorrow's shaft hath found unerring aim,
  And tears ensanguined blend in life's clear stream,
Each joy departing as in some spent dream,
While prayerless lips refuse all aid to claim,

Shall holy priest crush more that stricken frame?
  Reprove for beads untold, and harshly deem
  Religion deigns no more to light her beam
For one estranged, and thus giv'n o'er to blame?

Resign'd—but not the less with broken heart,
  The pensive mourner dwells on what hath been,
Nor solace findeth in the preacher's art.

  Excess of grief may oft like pride be seen,
Disdaining speech—with folded arms apart,
  Yet, communing with God in depths serene.

SONNET 3.

SWIFT is the bird uprising with the morn
    In orient grove at eve to safely sleep,
  Where with the rose his trysting-place to keep
He heeds not if his wing be travel-worn.

Unseen that land, and yet no flight forlorn—
    The lotus pool he knows, so calmly deep,
    By the pomegranate's shade where moonbeams creep,
There shall he be ere Dian wind her horn.

May *we* then shrink, less bold than he, the brave
    But fragile sailor of a pathless sky,
Nor dare the gale, and the wide gulf's storm-wave ?

    Or doubt of things veil'd briefly from our eye,
And, like the sluggard, rather slumber crave
    Than soar to Paradise exultingly !

SONNET 4.

AT sunrise wake the noisy hours of day,
　　Like courtiers clamorous for a monarch's smile,
　Or worldlings full of cunning and of guile,
Who strive for things which most the crowd may sway,

The marble halls, the singer's amorous lay,
　The pageant glittering, though beset with care,
　Their wealth a marvel in the zenith's glare,
Themselves the honour'd of the rich and gay.

The evening comes to find them left alone—
　Their gaudy idols fall with life's decline,
And mockery ascends the empty throne !

　Enamour'd now of loveliness divine,
A purer faith will for that love atone,
　Since joys immortal may with this combine.[1]

---

[1] The above is the arrangement of the lines in an edition of Pe-
trarch, *Venezia*, *M.D.L.X.* 4to. in 2 vols.

SONNET 5.

ALAS! shall we withhold the doubting smile
From those who find in life's wide wilderness
No deadly leaf—no bitter fruitfulness—
But shades where nestle serpents free from guile?

Without its thorn the rose might please awhile—
Though unmix'd pleasures here may never bless;
Soon all will perish that we most caress,
And thus to pain our thoughts we reconcile.

The first tear stealing down its novel course,
Fell for fair Eden's future waste and grief—
Upwelling from that deadly fount *Remorse!*

And now, what brings our utmost joy relief?
We find it not in maze of sweet discourse,
But 'tis the same! *tears,* passionate though brief.

SONNET 6.

I N youth, before the shades of doubt arose,
　　I found a garden deckt with many flow'rs,
　And hands beloved—for Love such art empowers—
A storied posy deftly did compose:

Fair blossoms there were chosen to disclose
　　Prophetic hues for happy future's hours,
　　And Clematis was pluck'd from woven bowers—
So fondly clinging to her untamed Rose.

Yet wherefore prize these wasting toys of Time?
　　The heart that sought them ne'er could fail or change,
Blooming more richly with the latest chime.

　　Undying love through Heaven's purest range
Best finds its nature amidst things sublime,
　　Whose rare perfection nothing can derange.

SONNET 7.

STORMS long had wrestled with the winter night,
  Nature distraught, and trembling with new fears,
  In disarray shed her neglected tears,
Deploring this, her sad and helpless flight.

Moonbeams burst forth, the mountain path in sight –
  The goatherd's voice his shaggy troop now cheers,
  He 'scapes the chasm which at his feet appears,
And bounding, turns to climb the rocky height.

Who hath not known unlook'd-for light like this,
  Rescue the thoughts that went to settled gloom,
Leading him far away from the abyss?

  Welcome such contrast to a low'ring doom :
With Peace once more returning with her kiss
  From the cold margin of her open tomb !

SONNET 8.

THOSE early pictures painted on the mind
    By Nature's love when in poetic vein,
From shocks of circumstance untouch'd remain,
No perish'd form—no tint to mould consign'd.

How swiftly-flew before a prospering wind
    The graceful sail that would our gaze retain
    By limpid shallows of the mighty main—
We see it all!—no faded beauty find.

Yon less'ning ship, so soon to disappear—
    Her prow sun-lit, or in the shadow cast,
Was it the image of our life's career?—

    From some fair hemisphere we thought it past
To one unknown—through trial sore to steer—
    With colours nail'd unto the straining mast !

SONNET 9.

L OUD boom'd the gun from forth the castle walls,
  War's peaceful message unto coming eve—
A stern farewell ! to him whose beams achieve
Their dazzling course ; and bright his armour falls.

The stars return—as when a truce recalls
  To sylvan scene the flocks that feuds aggrieve,
  And shepherds haste the secret fold to leave,
For meads where clarion-blast no more appals.

Hail hour of rest ! 'Tis now we cease to fret
  O'er dreaded partings, or for visions fled,
They came—they went—why tarries still regret ?

  One sun alone the hour's procession led,
One only love in one life's course was set—
  It lies enshrined beside the Holy Dead.

S

SONNET 10.

TO F. A. K.[1]

I F leaves of myrtle-sprigs of classic bay
    Could with their fragrance some sweet voice unite,
    I had not sought this sonnet to indite,
But left to them the homage of a lay.

The glist'ning myrtle in its green array
    Whilom found favour in your loving sight;
    Of bay-leaves Shakespeare[2] doth a legend cite;
Their leaves the Pythia's utterance could sway.[3]

In oracles I cannot speak my mind,
    You have won bays that are not of this gift—
Yet to indulgence be your heart inclined!

Of you my thoughts ne'er to decay could drift.
They in the Angel's plant[2] examples find
    That ever fresh doth verdant boughs uplift.

---

[1] With a bunch of myrtle and bay sprigs.

[2] See Notes to King Richard the Second, act 2, sc. iv. ed. 1793.

[3] The Pythian priestess chewed the leaves of the bay tree before she was placed on the sacred tripod. Hence the bay was called the Prophetic Tree. See Evelyn's *Silva*, 4to. York, ed. 1785, pp. 88-92.

SONNET 11.

MIDSUMMER EVENING AT ——, IN FRANCE.

FAR in that sky above my native shore,
    Behold Eve follows in the golden way
  Of her proud Lord !—gleaning each scatter'd ray,
To glad Earth's reapers now their toil is o'er !

Suffused with blushes, lovelier than before,
   She sadly leaves sweet summer's longest day,
  While with her Liege she wends from us away,
Ere Autumn come, and Winter cold and hoar.

A vision passes of departed joys,
   Crossing the brine from East to balmy West,
Ethereal forms no evil germ destroys ;

   They turn t'wards me a gaze of souls at rest,
Whose happy state no dark'ning doubt alloys,
  And pity one by mortal weight opprest.

SONNET 12.

TITIAN'S BIRTHPLACE.[1]

THE scene around was grandly desolate !
    Each Alp a fortress, from volcanic throes,
  Complete in strength, sent forth to challenge foes,
Or him to win whose birth they did await.

And to those Alps great Titian linked his fate,
    His canvas with their fascination glows ;
    In Venice, then—with friends his leisure chose—
Of them he spake in honour'd age sedate.

Ariosto, Sansovino—and all famed
    For talent not unworthy of such host,
The painter's friendship and his welcome claim'd.

    Queen of the Adriatic ! 'tis thy boast
To gather round thee all illustrious named,
    He of Cadore served ambition most.

---

[1] From the Campanile of St. Mark the Venetian Alps may be dis-
cerned above the waters of the Lagoons. The peak of Antelao, seventy
miles distant, towers over Cadore—Titian's birthplace. The repre-
sentation of nature first appears conceived with freedom and with
grandeur in the master-works of Titian, whose earlier studies were
among t those dolomitic cones. [See *Titian, his Life and Times,* by
Crowe and Cavalcaselle, 1877. Also *Cosmos,* vol. ii. p. 79.]

SONNET 13.

H E stood like one who gazes on a scene
　　To him endear'd, watching a vaporous cloud
　Curl o'er those woods that his own home enshroud,
Already felt the welcome true and keen.

Along the surge beneath was havoc seen,
　　And heard o'er rocks the billows crashing loud,
　　Like helpless deer, to death by hunters vow'd,
Bound to the covert where men have not been.

Fix'd was his eye—it had been baffled oft—
　　To where mists hid the fallen Pleiads' light,
Amidst her sisters shining pale and soft.

　　Her veil was caught by kindly winds in flight,
And him enwrapp'd whose arms were raised aloft ;
　　Day found him not—nor yet another night.

SONNET 14.

SOUL! part immortal of this mortal frame,
Fast are we bound together by strange ties,
A slave is each! each unto Freedom cries,
And thou, th' unseen, the mastery dost claim.

Into the world we gladiators came,
Not both to die—that we name *Life* the prize;
Hard is the struggle of the flesh—it dies—
The Victor thou!—such is at least thy fame.

Natheless, I know thee meddlesome to save,
From evil thou hast led me oft aside,
Though wayward I—and striving thee to brave.

Our destinies defy our towering pride.
Then Peace be heard! We part beside the grave,
And He above our merits must decide.

SONNET 15.

ETERNITY! familiar though strange word!
    Scarce is it other than an empty sound
That goes its way!—or, senseless echo found,
Returns once more with no new accents heard.

The limitless? our gauge of Time referr'd
    To distance known. Thought's widest, loftiest bound
    Fails helpless here, it sinks unto the ground,
Again to rise, again success deferr'd.

Eternity! irrevocable, stern—
    No clustering years that wear our lives away,
No promised end for which the suffering yearn!

    Yet—if it be a long, long happy day,
Without Farewells, and rich in joy's return,
    Who would not wish the Tyrant *Time's* decay?

SONNET 16.

THE words were said. He took the Friar's crown,
    Faint semblance of his Master's agony,
He will'd no sign should sacrifice imply,
And in his breast the rebel cry kept down.

His the Franciscan's simple robe of brown,
    Clothing his youthful limbs with poverty,
    The ardent glance of his wild eagle-eye
So upward fix'd; dispell'd his wonted frown.

Th' impassion'd strains in which his voice was heard
    Seem'd wing'd the range of ether to surmount,
With suppliant prayer to Paradise preferr'd.

    Yet came his thoughts from no unruffled Fount,
A something cross'd that had his mind disturb'd,
    He held his beads; but 'twas in vain to count.

SONNET 17.

POOR wind-rock'd leaf! I've watch'd thee droop
    alone,
  When all fair summer-friends forsook thine oak,
  And stems than thine more strengthful meanly broke,
And birds of song forsook thee one by one !

The ancient tree o'er which north blasts have gone,
  Thou wilt not leave, howe'er the storms provoke ;
  And for *his* sake dost pitying spring evoke,
No more for *thine*, thy cycling hours are done.

Thus rare that friend whose nobleness repels
  The thought to quit us when our winter falls,
And solitude of sorrow's sharpness tells,—

  Whom, like to thee, no adverse change appals,
But faithful proved, unto the long last dwells
  With what it loves,—so, fortune's day recalls.

IN THE CHAPEL OF SAINT SAUVEUR AT ——.

L IGHT of the World! whose faintest ray, too pure,
    Might sear the fountain of our feeble sight,
Before thine altar, oft in crypt obscure,
    A feeble flame burns through the day and night ;
Human the aid that kindles and sustains,
Exhausted else, all spent that lamp remains.

Redeemer and my God !—even for Thy sake
    I'd hail a symbol in itself that's fair,
Did I not mark the air's caprice doth make
    That flame subservient, and it trembleth there :
Inapt compàre to attribute of Thine—
Thine own effulgence, steadfast and divine !

THE OLD CHELSEA PENSIONERS.

THE muffled drum, the sharp and thrilling fife,
    Denote the march unto a soldier's grave:
The aged veteran, done with weary life,
    Is thither borne by comrades of the brave.

Nor their own summons shall they long await—
    The dashing daring that of manhood told
Gives place to feeble step and shuffling gait;
    They soon surrender, in Death's troop enroll'd.

If love, or gen'rous impulse, raised that pile,
    Above the Thames crowning its osier banks,
To curious search it scarce seems worth the while—
    The royal gift from England claims fair thanks.

Amidst its groves, within the guard-room walls,
    Peaceful alike, unstirr'd by war's alarms,
The ancient Pensioner his past recalls,
    Saunters, and prates of doughty deeds of arms.

Some moping sit, bent forward on their staff,
  Content to bask where sunshine may be found,
With vacant eye, perchance with childish laugh,
  Indifferent to all who pass around.

May be their pains in happy dreams they drown ;
  By cottage door achieve some childish feat ;
Or hear the shout to seek in fight renown :
  They wake to beating of the calm retreat.

Soon in each tranquil ward the lights are seen,
  And listless limbs and maim'd seek night's repose :
How rough soe'er the warrior's days have been,
  For him hath Chelsea shelter at their close !

NOTE.—A popular belief exists ascribing the erection of the Royal
Hospital, at Chelsea, to a suggestion made by Nell Gwynne to King
Charles II. that he should provide such an institution for the decayed
soldiers of his army.

TO M. R.

THERE was a time when side by side
  Our homes in tranquil beauty lay :
I see them still in all their pride—
  Restored by Fancy's playful sway.

It was not Nature's realm alone
  That gave this richness to my ken,
For Art, with graces of her own,
  A fresh delight would bring me then.

How oft beneath your father's roof
 I play'd a willing student's part—
Where note of praise or just reproof
 Won o'er the idlesse of my heart !

These lays, alas ! are little worth
 The welcome you bestow on them ;
Still they who give such trifles birth
 Feel silence more than words condemn.

Hath Music aught unto them lent ?—
 It is because she loved the theme,
And knew I sought her when I bent
 O'er rippling wave, and falling stream.

If now it fortune that I sing
 Where fair Indulgence proves less kind,
Harmless shall be the critic's sting
 When words of yours are brought to mind.

But there are themes held ever dear,
 By whomsoever they be sung.
The faulty chords may wound the ear,
 Yet laurels o'er the tale be flung.

Thus in obscurity came forth
 The tones that your sweet will doth praise,
Like merry dancers [1] of the North,
 Whose lightning in the twilight plays.

---

[1] The *aurora borealis*, so called in the Shetland Islands. (See *Come*, vol. i. p. 184.)

THE CURFEW-BELL AT PONT-L'ÉVÊQUE. [1]

A FRAGMENT.

" Put out the light, and then—Put out the light ?"
SHAKESPEARE. *Othello,* act v. sc. 2.

ONWARD—onward—dull mile still link'd to mile—
　　With travel's pleasure hard to reconcile—
Pursued by winds and wreaths of whirling dust,
　The Wanderer speeds whom days of winter trust.
It is too soon to seek the Norman shore
　Ere autumn's gale and hyemal frosts be o'er ;
Trust not the wave in earliest vernal morn,
　But wait for sign the white bloom of the thorn.

Then to the vessel's deck in haste repair,
　Breathe new existence—quaff the briny air,
Watch the sharp prow in gallant strength divide
　Wave after wave of the opposing tide.

---

[1] Pont-l'Évêque, Départ. Calvados, France. It is situated on the rivers Touques and Calonne.

Still hangs the mist about the chalky down
    And height to which the Poet gave renown,
The sea-gull, call'd by morning from the nest,
    On the blue deep displays his snowy breast.

Who that has steer'd past stern-faced La Joliette[1]
    Can soon, one feature in its scene forget—
The dazzling ring of those wild birds o'er head
    When o'er the narrow sea his galley sped.[2]

    *   *   *   *   *
    *   *   *   *   *
    *   *   *   *   *
    *   *   *   *   *

Delightful sense of freedom 'mid th' expanse[3]
    Of sky and sea that other joys enhance :
Our idlesse brief, with hope of pleasure rife,
    We give alone to the romance of life !
Too soon we bid the gentle sea farewell !
    So half inclined upon the main to dwell ;
The port is hail'd 'neath Gallia's sunny cliffs,
    'Tis time to glide beside the anchor'd skiffs.

---

[1] The new harbour at Marseilles, faced with magnificent masonry.
[2] The old port is entered through a narrow channel between the ancient castle of St. Jean and the fort St. Nicholas.
[3] . . . . "That which, by an expression of deep meaning, my native language terms *in das Freie* exercises a soothing and a calming influence on the sorrows and on the passions of man."—ALEX. HUMBOLDT, *Cosmos,* vol. i. P. S. Sabine's Trs.   London : Longmans, 1859.

'Tis now the month vow'd unto Heaven's Queen,
　Her shrines are deck'd with lilies fairest seen.
No vesper-hour but hears the hymn upraised,
　Her aid invoked—her holy virtues praised.
There is new life upspringing everywhere,—
　The fields, for autumn harvest-homes prepare ;
They bring forth many from the selfsame field—
　Our years but *one*—immortal grain to yield.

Amidst grey walls climb favourites of age,
　Young tendrils prone to claim their heritage.
In crevice deep or bastion fall'n away,
　They, never daunted, urge their winning way.
Now comes the flock to narrow pastures led,
　Check'd by the watch-dog if it dare to spread,
While on the bank his master stretch'd at ease
　Around him folds his shaggy coat of frieze.

Yet not Arcadia's sylvan land is this,
　Idyllic charms we are constrain'd to miss :
Yon shepherd's pipe, unlike the classic reed,
　Exhales no music o'er the grassy mead.
And where are they of Nature's primal choir ?
　The woods in vain the warbling notes desire.
Doth silence then more fitly mourning dwell ?
　If page historic sternest truth must tell

How by the castle's walls, not far remote,
　The cannon's lightning first the foeman smote.

L

And France awoke to hear the deaf'ning roar
   Of Mars' last gift to crown the brow of war.[1]

      *   *   *   *   *

      *   *   *   *   *

      *   *   *   *   *

      *   *   *   *   *

When summer days their genial task fulfil,
   When clouds are gone, and night forgets to chill,
See youth come forth from lowly village cot
   With song and dance to cheer their humble lot.
Sweet is the song that pretty Annette sings,
   Swift to her side it faithful Lubin brings,
And e'er they dance the cowslip mead along
   'Mid shouts the lover crowns her Queen of Song !

A very sylph among a sturdier race—
   The sculptor's model in her native grace :
A mind as fair doth her dark eye disclose
   Whate'er the mood—in action or repose.
Not many those—wayfarers though in haste—
   Who will not halt this rustic mirth to taste ;
Some nimbly join and foot it in the ring,
   To Annette some the choicest posy bring.

Such was the season when at Pont-l'Evêque,
   A stranger chanced a journey's halt to make.

---

[1] " Pont-Audemer, fière de son château au siége duquel, pour la
première fois en France, on se servit de canons, et qui fut rasé par
Duguesclin, en 1378."—*Essai sur l'arrondissement de Pont-Audemer,
par A. Canel,* 1833, &c.

The modest inn could serve him at his need,
   Though poor acceptance both for man and steed.
The wooden bench outside the vine-wreathed door,
   Cool'd by the bough of elm or sycamore;
The draught of cider in capacious glass
   Sufficed for most who there might choose to pass.

An hour it was for lonely musing made,
   The town, the river, sinking into shade;
Above, the noiseless flight of homing-bird,
   The curfew-bell for solemn music heard.
Eve closed her lattice in the pearly west
   From whence had stream'd the blush her love confest.
Day's closing eye beheld the Crescent's light
   Guide on their path the handmaids of the night.

Retiring slow, as on each bright Star came
   Bearing the measureless far-flashing flame
That groups of myriad years saw fly to Earth,[1]
   We count them not—that labour ends in dearth!
Titanic thought!—and yet—and yet—how mounts
   The soul of man to those unfathom'd founts,
On wings that spurn the leaden nether air,
   To claim existence in those worlds so fair!

---

[1] . . . . " According to the knowledge we possess of the velocity of light, it is more than probable that the light of the most distant cosmical bodies offers us the oldest sensible evidence of the existence of matter."—*Cosmos*, vol. i. p. 145.

This planet sinks, with all its paltry strife,
　　And all the hoards that make its petty life ;
Love—love alone, unvarnish'd reappears
　　Safe in its home, the pure immortal spheres !—
Around the wand'rer fascination wove
　　That subtle spell which bids our thoughts to rove,
He cross'd the arch and reach'd Walhalla's halls,
　　And saw the fortune which the Blest befalls. [1]

The night wore on and long had set the moon,
　　And yet for sleep it still appear'd too soon.
The stranger from the outer prospect turn'd,
　　But rest came not, though well it had been earn'd.
No stage more fit for fancy's play design'd
　　Than the rude garret to this guest assign'd,
With tap'stry hung, all faded and half rent,
　　The oaken planks beneath his footsteps bent.

What did he care ?　Many a worse had been
　　A welcome resting-place in foreign scene.
Some influence now had changed to gloom his mood,
　　And forms uncall'd for—shades before him stood.
Are not impressions forced upon our mind,
　　Against our will, that we prophetic find ?
That cast a wan pale light on coming things ?
　　Too oft on Happiness with parting wings !

---

[1] The fabled rainbow which leads to Walhalla, the Scandinavian
Paradise.

Before his view there loom'd the Gothic tower,
   Which so impress'd him in his boyish hour,
When quick to note the wile of placid mask
   They wore, who answer'd what he dared to ask.
And well remember'd when he clomb the stair
   A door flew wide, moved by some gust of air,
And instinct, shudd'ring, told that *Death* was there,
   Who? what? no whisper'd voice to say would dare!

None came the midnight lamp for *him* to trim,
   He felt, not saw, the steps to attic dim
Where from his cot he watch'd the moonbeams wane
   Athwart the deep stone-mullion'd window-pane
As sway'd and rock'd the shadowy yew-trees nigh,
   And something sigh'd, or seem'd at least to sigh,
While branches quivering, quaintly-shaped and small,
   Like human fingers wrote upon the wall.

Wakeful, he heard the passage clock tick clear,
   And that strange noise he heard of owlets[1] near—
As breath of giants in a quiet sleep—
   With meted pause that rhythm true might keep;

---

[1] Bewick attributes this noise to the white owl—*strix flammea*—when he refers to its resemblance to hard breathing in human beings. Mudie, in his "Feathered Tribes," following the celebrated naturalist Warburton, says it is the plaint of the young owls for food. The singular sound attracted the attention of Sir David Wilkie during the visits this distinguished painter made to the father of the author, who frequently accompanied him to the adjoining cliffs on summer evenings, on purpose to listen to the sound which fascinated him.

And then, no wonted task with daylight came,
　　The play-time pass'd without its merry game ;
Summon'd at length, he wondering stared around
　　Where ev'ry look seem'd rooted to the ground.

'Mid silent groups, all robed in black attire,
　　Silent there sat his stern and agèd sire ;
With childhood's eager eye as half in pain,
　　The boy his playmate sought—he sought in vain !
The vision closed.[1]

```
   *      *      *      *      *

   *      *      *      *      *

   *      *      *      *      *
```

Years have gone by, and it is spring once more,
　　The Ides of March come fatal as of yore !
No sign betrays that youth is drawing near
　　All garland-crown'd so soon to reappear.
For on the upland slope the golden grain
　　Earth's miser clutch awhile will yet retain,
From eastern steppe low moans the blighting wind
　　Fast in its cell each tender bud to bind.

---

[1] "It is an old tradition that spirits were relieved from the confine-
ment in which they were held during the day at the time of curfew,
that is at the close of day, and were permitted to wander at large till
the first cock-crowing. Hence in *The Tempest* they are said to 'rejoice
to hear the solemn curfew.'"—MALONE, note to act 3, scene iv.
"Plays of William Shakespeare," with notes by Johnson, Steevens,
Malone, and others.

The giant trees adown the avenue—
  All seasons' slaves! wear on the winter's hue,
As they who long the weeds of grief have worn
  Pause ere they change, lest deem'd they cease to mourn!
Behold a long procession wind its way
  In sorrow's vain, poor meaningless array!
How jars that pomp when they, alas! who love,
  Sigh for the desert of the lonely dove ;

The precious burden slowly borne along
  Through leafless aisles, with tears and sobs for song.
In sacred rest doth bear that envied part—
  Whate'er it be—we can to none impart.

        *   *   *   *   *
        *   *   *   *   *
        *   *   *   *   *
        *   *   *   *   *

The Wanderer? doth he now hear that knell?
  'Tis not the voice of the old Norman bell
In belfry swinging high, and at whose feet
  The streams of Touques and of Calonne meet?
Enough!—it is the language of command—
  His heart obeys, no matter in what land.
Smite not the bell again, for *it is night*,
  Darkness o'er all—*Death hath put out the light.*

MORNING. NOON. NIGHT.

IN MEMORY OF * * *

* * * "Nessun maggior dolore,
Che ricordarsi del tempo felice
Nella miseria." * * * * * *
* * * * * * * * * * *

"Farò come colui, che piange e dice."—DANTE.

FOND conceit ! that Death
    could dare inweave
In his dark web the pow'r thy
    name to leave
'Midst things that drift away at
    his decree !
      Shall I not think of Thee ?

The wreath that deck'd thy bier
    but one poor day
Fades in the vault—hid from the
    sun-lit ray,—
May not these words a living tribute be ?
    Shall I not think of Thee ?

We were together in our youth's fresh morn,
Whose hours refused—though at red-sunrise born—
To cease their song, or dark'ning eve foresee!
    Shall I not think of Thee?

Each season left some sweet and storied leaf—
Memorials pluck'd to tell with joy or grief
How once they grew on life's fair-planted tree,—
    Shall I not think of Thee?

In shadeless noon, when bird and beast lie still—
When labour rests beside the cooling rill
That leaps from rock to rock in childish glee,
    Shall I not think of Thee?

Our noontide bow'r, alas! beheld cold shade
Defeat the summer all our gladness made,
And joy depart as birds from winter flee—
    Shall I not think of Thee?

When night disarms the hurtling hours to give
Enchanting peace brief space with us to live,
And fretful day we cease to hear or see,
    Shall I not think of Thee?

In sorrow's night I summon back the days
When hand in hand through pleasant blithesome ways
None ever sweeter counsel took than we—
    Shall I not think of Thee?

        X

Within those walls where oft we knelt in pray'r,
Say, gentle Spirit! art thou—unseen—there?
When in devotion wrapt I bend the knee,
    Shall I not think of Thee?

Thou answ'rest not! Would it were mine to hear
As in the past thy voice still banish fear,
And with my faith its harmony agree—
    Shall I not think of Thee?

That bitter word—farewell!—dies on my lip.
Have we not still some fair companionship?
Or if not yet—Time's wings will set me free—
    Shall I not follow Thee?

SONNET.

FORTH on the world these pages take their way
   To meet the stranger's—not unfriendly eye?
  Like better things they may neglected lie—
To Fashion worthless—and for Time a prey.

Shall *some* still read them, dreaming of a day
   When they too sought the muse of poesy,
   And joy'd to dwell 'mid some fair scenery
With loves and friendships that have passed away?

From such as these the judgment may be kind—
   And more than this should my proud thought desire?
Though other voices faintly fall behind.

Full many a joy were doom'd to soon expire,
That lives while fost'ring beams surround the mind,
   If Scorn alone breathed on the humble lyre.

THE LAST FAREWELL.

FAREWELL! we part!—it will, and must be so,
    Ere yet these moments we had learnt to fear!
They seem'd so distant and so full of woe,
    Our minds shrank from the task to bring them near.

Farewell!—a world is circled by that sound—
  A changèd world henceforth through one distress
Where wasting thoughts will comfortless abound,
  And mask'd in silence never grieve the less.

Farewell!—let sweet forgiveness calm this hour!
  If ever I have stray'd from love to thee—
If e'er a look—a word—to wound had power—
  I kneel before thee: dost thou pardon me?

Farewell!—could speech say more it were but pain:
  It shrinks from truth—it cannot falsehood tell.
I feel to marble turn my heart—my brain!—
  Dost Thou *still* hear? Oh, then, once more, Farewell!

www.ingramcontent.com/pod-product-compliance
Lightning Source LLC
Chambersburg PA
CBHW030900050726
47500CB00009B/551